OPERATION SABRE

A PAUL FOX SPY ADVENTURE

GLENN CARTER

*To my wife Anna and my three daughters
Maria, Eva and Lydia.*

I love you more than I can express.

1

THE WHEEL

PAUL FOX SEES things that others don't, and today was no exception.

It was Christmas Eve and Paul was walking west against the bitterly cold wind. He was on Princes Street in Edinburgh with his twin sister Rachel and his friend Sharav. Paul and Rachel had expected to meet their dad at Waverley train station, but after waiting for over an hour, they had given up.

The three 12-year-olds had been walking for a couple of minutes when Paul suddenly turned around and walked in the opposite direction.

'What is it?' Rachel called out as she grabbed Sharav, pulling him after her.

'Something's not right,' Paul said, pointing at the back of a male teenager dressed in black, fifty metres in front of them.

'Oh, not again!' sighed Rachel.

A minute earlier Paul had noticed the teenager walking towards them. He couldn't quite explain it, but something had made him suspicious. Something about how he was walking, the tension in his face and the size of his bag.

Sharav looked confused. 'Why are we going this way?'

'Oh, it's just another of Paul's delusional fantasies,' Rachel replied.

'I just want to follow him for a minute,' said Paul, scanning the horizon.

They were approaching the big wheel in Princes Street Gardens. A shiny Jaguar car and two Land Rovers were parked nearby, surrounded by several smartly dressed men. Paul felt his heart race. 'This isn't good,' he said and started running towards the security guards.

The Prime Minister was visiting Scotland and she was taking the opportunity for a photoshoot in Princes Street Gardens. As Paul approached the gates, he noticed the Prime Minister smiling broadly as she got on to the big wheel with a bodyguard. The youth whom Paul had followed was getting into the pod behind them. At that moment the array of Christmas lights, the heady scents of hot chocolate and ginger-bread and the joyful sound of carollers all faded as Paul locked on to the threat. Fuelled by adrenaline, Paul ran up to the kiosk and paid £5 for a ticket. There was a small voice inside Paul warning caution. 'No' said Paul out loud, 'not this time.' He pushed the caution aside. Paul felt an overwhelming desire to save and protect and although he couldn't control it, he knew why it was there. It had been there for two years now.

Paul climbed onto the big wheel; his eyes fixed on the teenager four pods above him. Edinburgh's big wheel stood forty-five metres tall and had twenty-five pods in total. Sporting a red and white vintage design, each pod, whilst open to the elements, had a roof and white metal barriers surrounding the occupants. Paul kept his eyes on the teenager who had his head down, searching in his bag. The wheel was moving gradually upwards as the operators let more people on at the bottom. Paul's eyes widened as he saw the teenager pull from his bag what seemed to be a toy gun. He then pointed the gun towards the Prime Minister and her bodyguard. Nothing happened at first, but after fifteen seconds the bodyguard stood up abruptly and looked around. He then started frantically patting himself down as if he was on fire, but there were no flames. The PM stood up and reached towards the bodyguard in alarm. Paul knew that he had to do something. 'Got to get up there,' he said as he pulled out his pen knife and forced the lock on the door of the pod. He sensed the danger, but the fear was overridden by the compulsion to protect. All he cared about was saving the Prime Minister. Paul threw himself upwards and slammed against the next pod, just managing to grab onto the middle railing.

The teenager continued to train the gun on the bodyguard, who was now panicking. He was pulling hard on the door of the pod, frantically trying to escape. Finally, the door opened, and he flung himself towards the pod below, which broke his fall. He then fell a further twenty metres and landed on the roof of the ticket kiosk. As soon as the bodyguard had been neutralised, the teenager put the gun away and started climbing towards the Prime Minister. Paul had to move quickly.

The big wheel had stopped, and the Prime Minister was right at the top. Paul looked down. Chaos.

Parents gathering children into their arms, people running in different directions, screaming and trampling those who had fallen over. The security detail knew there was a threat to the Prime Minister, and they were radioing for back-up. The teenager had reached the Prime Minister and was climbing into her pod. Paul was almost there. He made his final jump to reach the pod. There was a flash of metal as the teenager lunged towards the PM with a weapon. Paul landed heavily against the railing. The teenager, startled by Paul's appearance, took a step back. Paul grabbed at the legs of the attacker and knocked him off his feet. With one fluid movement Paul pulled himself up and into the pod. The PM was slumped in a seat, breathing heavily. Paul grabbed for the knife, but the teenager swiftly landed a punch to Paul's right temple, knocking him down. Paul slowly stood up. His head was ringing. He caught sight of the teenager's legs as he climbed out of the pod and up onto the roof.

Paul pulled off his jacket and rolled it into a ball. Giving it to the Prime Minister he said, 'Press this onto your arm.' With that he turned and started to climb after the attacker. He was soon standing precariously on the roof of the pod. The dark figure had his back to Paul and was unfolding something that looked like a large kite. Paul realised it was a compact, black glider, about eight feet across. He was preparing to jump. As he was holding the glider above his head, Paul rushed forward and grabbed him from behind. They toppled off the big wheel together and flew in the direction of the Scott Monument. Paul held on firmly as the wind rushed past them. There was a huge tree between them and the monument. The teenager just about managed to navigate around it. Their descent was fast. This glider was clearly not designed for two.

Rachel and Sharav had watched all of this from below and were sprinting after the glider. In the commotion some children had left their BMX bikes unattended, so Rachel and Sharav grabbed the bikes and started pedalling furiously in the direction of the glider, past the running bodyguards and towards the monument. They arrived just in time to see the teenager running away from Paul who was lifeless on the ground. Rachel threw the BMX to the side and crouched down beside Paul, shaking him to see if he was okay.

'I'm okay, I'm okay. Get him!' said Paul.

'Okay then,' said Rachel, sounding unsure.

Rachel and Sharav pedalled after the assailant who was running fast despite a limp. Rachel passed the teenager and slammed on her front brake. The bike went into a front wheelie and with one quick movement, Rachel swung the back wheel around, hitting the teenager hard on the side of his head and slamming him into the path. He was knocked out cold. Sharav jumped off his bike and sat on the young man.

The bodyguards arrived a minute later. One of them nodded towards Sharav and asked Rachel, 'Is he okay?' Rachel realised Sharav was snoring quietly, and she smiled, saying, 'Yeah, it's a long story but when he gets overexcited, he sometimes sleeps.' The bodyguard raised his eyebrows, slowly rolled Sharav to one side, and handcuffed the unconscious teenager.

2

RECRUITS

PAUL, RACHEL AND Sharav spent the next hour being debriefed on the steps of the Scott Monument by two friendly, plain-clothes detectives called Natalie and Rob.

'Tell me about that gun again?' asked Natalie. Paul described the gun's features and how the bodyguard had acted when it was pointed at him.

'Sounds like it might be an ADS,' said Rob, who had a gentle Edinburgh accent.

'Yes, but they are normally mounted on tanks!' exclaimed Natalie. 'I've never seen technology like that in such a small firearm.'

'ADS?' asked Rachel.

'Oh sorry,' said Rob. 'ADS stands for Active Denial System. It's a non-lethal weapon designed by the Americans and basically works like a high frequency microwave. It's also known as the "heat ray". It heats the surface of the target. Really unpleasant, like being cooked I suppose.'

'Oh, that's terrible!' said Sharav.

'How's the Prime Minister?' asked Paul.

'They've rushed her to the Royal Infirmary, but the last we heard she was trying to organise her next engagement,' smiled Natalie. 'Unbelievable, really.'

AS NATALIE AND Rob finished the debrief, Natalie asked them whether they would like a lift home.

Paul shook his head and said, 'Thanks, but we'll make our own way home. We need to pick something up at Sharav's place anyway.'

'You sure?' said Natalie, fixing Paul with a hard stare.

Paul shifted uncomfortably from one foot to another, 'Yes, we'll be fine.'

'Okay then. Listen, if you remember anything else then please contact me. I'll give you my card.'

Natalie handed each of them a card. The card felt cold and heavy in Paul's hand. He looked down and saw that it was made of black metal with a simple 'MI2' emblazoned on the front.

Paul looked up and was about to ask a question,

but Natalie and Rob were already ten metres away.

THE TEENAGERS SET off and walked across the Old Town to get to their bus stop. They chose to take a short cut down one of Edinburgh's closes that linked Victoria Street with the Cowgate.

'I hate these closes!' exclaimed Sharav.

Paul smiled, 'I thought it would give you a bit of a thrill.'

'But they are dark, the walls can't be a metre and a half apart and they smell of pee—eek!'

Sharav's complaint ended in a high-pitched scream that was cut short.

Paul and Rachel swung round to see Rob holding his hand over Sharav's mouth. Sharav's eyes were bulging as he tried to look behind him. Rob slowly took his hand away from Sharav's mouth.

'Natalie, Rob…' Paul said. 'You gave us such a fright.'

'I now understand why the closes smell like pee,' Sharav smiled sheepishly.

'Sorry, you three,' said Natalie quietly. 'We wanted to finish our conversation.'

'I thought our conversation was finished,' said

Rachel.

'Well, yes but there was something else we wanted to talk about, and we couldn't do it in such a public place,' smiled Rob. 'Sorry about grabbing you Sharav, I was trying to avoid a scene.'

'It's fine, apologies for the scream.'

Natalie's eyes narrowed, 'Listen, you all helped to save the Prime Minister's life today. Rob and I aren't detectives. We are actually intelligence agents for MI5. We followed you because we wanted to ask you all something. We need young people like you to counter the threat we are facing to our national security.'

Rachel pulled out the metal card, 'What is MI2?' she asked.

Rob replied, 'MI2 originally handled Russian and Scandinavian Intelligence after the first world war but its functions were absorbed by MI3 in 1941. We have resurrected the name and now it's basically the youth division of MI5. Its primary purpose is to keep the country safe.'

Paul looked directly at Rachel as he felt the excitement build inside him. He saw her eyebrows furrow and the faintest movement of her head from left to right. He knew what she was thinking and then she said it.

'No, Paul. Don't you dare.'

'Let's just hear what they have to say,' responded Paul.

Natalie continued, 'There are increasing numbers of teenagers being radicalised in the UK and as you saw today, they are extremely dangerous. They have access to the latest technology and sophisticated weapons systems. We are recruiting teenagers like you to combat this threat and, if required, to infiltrate these cells. You would receive excellent training and development at our HQ in London. We try to fit most of the training within school holidays, although there is some time off school required.'

Paul and Sharav's eyes lit up at the thought of time off school.

'But you will be required to do additional school studies at headquarters,' Rob said with a grin.

Rachel shook her head, 'That all sounds very worthwhile, but we have a lot going on at the moment and we have school to think about.'

Sharav said, 'Yeah, and I've got this medical condition called narcolepsy. I've had it since I was 10. It basically means I can fall asleep suddenly during the day. I get hallucinations and just fall down randomly. I don't think I would be much use to a spy agency.'

'Yes, I noticed your condition,' said Natalie, 'but you did a fine job today despite all that.' She turned to Paul, 'What are you thinking, Paul?'

Rachel stared at Paul, nervously holding her breath.

Paul sighed, letting go of the opportunity and said, 'Eh, I think Rachel is right. We have a lot going on at the moment. My dad is away a lot and we have to look out for our mum.'

Natalie nodded, 'Okay, that's totally fine. If you change your mind you can sign up using that business card I gave you.'

Rob shook hands with each of them, saying, 'It was good to meet you three. You have done the country a great service today.'

3

CHRISTMAS

PAUL, RACHEL AND Sharav travelled on the bus in silence. Paul's thoughts turned to Christmas. He recalled last Christmas and how he had spent the majority of the day in his room. His chest tightened as a sense of sadness began to take hold. The memory was only softened by the fact that Sharav needed somewhere to stay this year. They had only known each other for four months since starting secondary school, but it felt like much longer. Paul glanced at Sharav and was instantly put at ease.

Rachel went on ahead, as Paul and Sharav took a detour to pick up Sharav's suitcase at his auntie's.

'So, how far away is your house?' asked Sharav.

'Couple of miles away.'

'Oh,' Sharav said, looking down at his huge suitcase. 'Are we walking?'

'Yep!'

'Better get started then.'

The boys took turns to drag the enormous suit-case the two miles, mostly uphill, to Paul's house. As they neared the house several snowflakes fell in front of them. The boys smiled at each other.

'That's my house,' said Paul, pointing at the only house in the cul-de-sac without Christmas lights. The Foxes' house was dark and the garden looked wild and unkempt. Paul noticed Sharav staring at the house and thought he'd better say something. 'Listen Sharav, there's something you probably need to know.'

Sharav raised his eyebrows. 'What's that?'

Paul stopped walking and rubbed his hands to-gether, trying to muster the courage to speak. 'Well… I've been meaning to tell you, it's just… well, it hasn't really come up.'

'You're actually a girl?' smiled Sharav.

Paul laughed and then looked down. 'No, a cou-ple of years ago my sister died in a car accident. The brakes in the car failed. Her name was Kate and she was six at the time.' He paused, struggling to get the next sentence out. He coughed and then said, 'The reason you need to know is that my mum and dad are really different now… sadder. You know, since she died.'

Sharav said, 'I'm so sorry, that's terrible.'

'Yeah it is,' said Paul, rubbing his eyes. Paul stood up straight in an attempt to ward off the sadness. 'It's not so bad, Dad buys me lots of technology because he feels guilty for spending so much time away from home.' Paul reached into his pocket and pulled out the latest iPhone.

'Sweet,' said Sharav.

PAUL WOKE AT 8.30 am to a strange noise outside. He staggered over to the window, rubbing the sleep from his eyes and squinting out at the morning light. To his surprise the bright sun was reflecting off a new covering of snow. As far as his eyes could see, the neighbourhood had been transformed. It was clean and crisp under a foot of snow. He smiled as he noticed that he had been woken up by a couple of younger kids next door, who were cycling their new bikes into a small snowdrift.

'Oh, it's Christmas,' he said out loud.

Sharav was still fast asleep. Paul remembered Sharav saying that he could sleep through anything and his parents often had to use extreme measures to wake him up.

'Okay then, extreme measures it is,' thought Paul. He pulled on some trousers, a warm jumper and trainers and ran downstairs. He returned two minutes later with three snowballs, which he threw at Sharav's head. Sharav only stirred after the second snowball brushed his nose. He woke with a start as the third snowball hit his ear.

'Ohhh, what… it's raining. Oh, it's really cold.'

'Morning, Sharav. Happy Christmas. Guess what happened outside?'

'Ehh, it's raining? Earthquake? Wait… oh snow?'

'Yes,' laughed Paul. 'It snowed last night. And you've just been woken up by three snowballs. First time that ever happened?'

'Yep, first time,' Sharav smiled as he dried his face with the duvet, 'Happy Christmas, Paul.'

'Happy Christmas,' said Paul brightly.

Sharav shivered. 'Ugh, a snowball in the ear isn't the best way to be woken up. It's not the worst, though! My brother once woke me up with a snake in my bed.'

Sharav rummaged under the bed and pulled out a

long, strangely shaped object that had been wrapped in brown paper. 'I've got you a present. Sorry about the wrapping.'

'Don't apologise, it's the present that counts,' Paul said, pulling off the paper to reveal the biggest Toblerone he had ever seen. 'It's huge!' Paul smiled as he ripped open the cardboard and threw two large chunks to Sharav.

'Yum,' said Sharav as he crammed a piece into this mouth.

The boys ate through half of the Toblerone and only stopped when the nausea set in.

'Oh, I've got a present for you.' Paul hesitated. 'I'm really sorry, it's terrible.'

'I'm sure it's not that bad,' said Sharav.

'No really, it is.' Paul handed the present to Sharav, noting that some snow had landed on it and soaked through the paper. Sharav opened it and smiled. 'It's a… it's a facecloth, a brown facecloth.' He smiled as he looked up from the facecloth at Paul, whose eyebrows were raised.

'Yeah, a soggy brown facecloth,' said Paul. Sharav began to laugh and then so did Paul. And then something happened to Paul, something that hadn't happened in long time. Paul laughed and laughed until his sides hurt and he found it difficult to breathe. Both boys were rolling around the floor unable to control themselves for about five minutes, until Paul couldn't take it anymore and crawled out of the room. He sat in the hall, trying to breathe deeply. He would occasionally start laughing again when he heard Sharav howling in the bedroom and saying 'soggy facecloth' to himself.

THE BOYS EVENTUALLY composed themselves and got dressed. They went downstairs and ate some breakfast with Rachel in the kitchen. At about 10 am Mrs Fox entered the room. She tried to smile, but it was obvious that she had been crying. 'Good morning dears, Happy Christmas.'

Rachel gave her mum a hug and said, 'Happy Christmas, Mum.'

'Happy Christmas, Mrs Fox,' said Sharav.

'Happy Christmas, Mum,' said Paul, as he went over and gave her a big hug. She held on to him.

'Where's Dad?' asked Paul.

'I'm not sure,' replied his Mum anxiously. 'He's still not back. He's never been away on Christmas

Day before. Perhaps there's some crisis at the European Council. I'm sure he'll be here soon.'

'Right,' said Paul unconvinced.

'Mum, can we go through to the living room and give out some presents?' asked Rachel, trying to sound upbeat.

'Yes dear, let me give your Uncle Stewart a phone just to see if he knows where your dad is.'

Paul, Rachel and Sharav went through to the living room and turned on the Christmas tree lights. The tiny, scraggly tree looked pathetic in the light of day.

Mrs Fox came in and sat down in a chair beside the Christmas tree, where she could look out the window.

'Any news from Uncle Stewart?' Rachel asked, her face colouring.

'No, he says he hasn't heard anything either, but that he would make a few calls to see if he can track him down.'

Paul stood up and walked towards the tree, saying, 'Right Mum, I've got you a present.' He picked up her present and handed it over, followed by a kiss on the cheek.

'Thank you, love.' She slowly unwrapped the present to reveal a perfume bottle. 'Oh, lovely.'

'Yeah, it's eh… expensive,' smiled Paul.

'Thank you dear, thank you very much.'

Sharav also handed a present to Mrs Fox and said, 'Oh this is from me and my parents, just to thank you for having me to stay and cause, well, because it's Christmas.'

'Oh, you shouldn't have, Sharav,' said Mrs Fox catching his eye.

'It's nothing, it's just small.'

Mrs Fox unwrapped the small present to reveal a simple wooden carving of a parent hugging a child. She stared at the carving for about ten seconds, making Sharav think that she really didn't like it. Then, slowly, a single tear fell on the gift.

Sharav looked at Paul, alarmed, and Paul mouthed silently, 'It's fine.'

Paul put his hand on his Mum's shoulder, 'You okay, Mum?'

'Yes, it's, it's beautiful.'

'Okay, right, well I wonder if there are any other presents under the tree.'

They exchanged some more gifts and Paul put on

a brave face to hide his disappointment at getting a new jumper, socks and some chocolate Santas. Sharav opened some presents from his parents that included some money, a book about God and a boomerang. 'We could do some damage with that!' Paul laughed as he pretended to throw it at the window.

Rachel excelled at present giving. She gave her mum and Paul a couple of beautifully wrapped gifts. She even managed to get headphones for Sharav. Rachel looked at her father's unopened present and put her hand on her stomach. Paul looked at Rachel. They all felt it. Where was Michael Fox?

4

THE CALL

PAUL AND RACHEL managed to cook a reasonable Christmas dinner. Everyone stoically ate the over-cooked turkey and Sharav even managed to say that it was 'moist'. He had picked up the word from previous Christmases. All adults said turkey was 'moist'.

There was still no news from Mr Fox, so at 3 pm, as the light was beginning to fade, Paul suggested that they go out for a walk. Mrs Fox, having already left several messages on her husband's voicemail and spoken to Stewart a couple more times, said that she would prefer to stay at home and wait for Michael to call. So the three young people headed out in the snow towards Pepper Wood.

The streets were deserted as families throughout the village were indoors watching old Christmas films and overeating cheap chocolate. The snow had a deadening effect on the noise. 'It's so quiet,' said Rachel. They looked around as the soft light of the sun slowly began to set.

As they walked through the wood, Sharav entertained Rachel and Paul with stories of Christmases gone by. He described the different Christmas traditions in a range of exotic locations around the world.

'Yeah and in Caracas in Venezuela the streets are closed to cars in the morning, so hundreds of people can roller-skate to mass! I joined in but crashed into a static granny. She was fine, but I wasn't! Quite a lot of blood.'

Just then they were startled by a female jogger who passed them at pace. She was a few metres in front of them when she dropped something. Paul ran forward to pick it up. It was a £2 coin. He called out to her, 'Excuse me, you've dropped something!' The jogger continued running. Paul shrugged his shoulders and put the coin in his pocket.

Towards the end of their walk Paul took the coin out of his pocket and studied it under the light of a lamppost. 'It's odd. Why would someone be running at that time on Christmas Day?'

'There are some crazy exercise people out there, Paul,' said Rachel. 'Some of them can't go a day without a run.'

'Yeah but there's something not right with this coin. It's too light.'

'Paul, it's freezing out here,' said Sharav. 'Can we go inside?'

Paul knocked the coin on the lamppost and then tried to twist it. To their astonishment he began to untwist the top of the coin. Inside the hollow coin was a carefully folded piece of paper with some printed text. Paul read it out.

'Your father has been captured and he is in grave danger. If you want to save him, agree to the recruitment and get to MI2 headquarters as soon as you can. Uncover the double agent. There are dangerous people who will try to stop you at all costs. Destroy this message.'

Paul and Rachel stared at each other, speechless. After a few moments Sharav piped up, 'That's… weird.'

Rachel said, 'Why would anyone want to capture our dad? He's a civil servant. He's not important!'

Paul's head swam and his mouth became dry. He eventually spoke with determination in his eyes, 'This makes sense. Dad wouldn't miss Christmas. I've been feeling it all day. Something bad has happened and we have to help him. We don't have a choice.'

'Let's go to the police. They'll help!' said Sharav.

'No way,' said Paul. 'We can't trust anyone, and the security services are way more powerful than the police. If anyone finds out about this, it could make things worse for Dad and us.'

They huddled together and, one after the other, pulled out the MI2 business cards.

'Hmm, there are no contact details on the card. How are we supposed to contact Natalie and Rob?' Rachel asked, looking at Paul.

'Yeah, no bar code, no chip. They are pretty heavy, though,' said Paul.

'I wonder,' Rachel said as she reached into her coat and took out her phone. She gently touched her phone with the card and smiled as they heard a gentle 'bing'. A black coloured app started to download. The sign-up process didn't take long, in fact all they had to do was type in their name, take a photo of themselves and tick a box. As they headed home Paul heard a notification. He looked down at his phone and read out the message:

'Thank you for signing up. There is one final step before your recruitment is confirmed. Please get to this location in 20 minutes. We will not wait.'

Paul looked, wide eyed, at the map. Both Rachel and Sharav had received the same message.

'That's Dundas Estate! It's directing us to a tennis court. Does Dundas Castle have a tennis court?'

'Looks like it,' said Rachel.

'We've got to get there fast. It's 1.5 miles from here. We'll need to run,' said Paul with urgency.

'Oh, not running,' exclaimed Sharav. 'Can we get a taxi?'

'Not on Christmas night, Sharav!' smiled Paul.

FIFTEEN MINUTES LATER, the group was approaching Dundas Castle. The grey brick castle rose from the well-kept lawn like a magnificent ship on a still sea.

Paul was pushing Sharav from behind and Rachel was dragging him from the front.

'Almost there,' puffed Paul.

'Oh dear, we can't go any further,' said Sharav, pointing at the 'Private Property' sign.

'Listen Sharav, if we're going to join MI2, we're going to have to break some rules,' Paul pointed out.

Rachel glanced at her phone. 'Just over this hill.'

They reached the tennis court just in time to hear a strange buzzing noise. Soon they saw three red flashing lights heading towards them at speed. 'Drones!' exclaimed Paul. 'Look, Sharav!'

Paul turned around to see Sharav fast asleep in a snowdrift.

The drones hovered ten feet above their heads and gradually descended, landing on the court. To their astonishment the drones deposited three packages before rising up and disappearing towards the bridges over the Forth.

THE PACKAGES WERE labelled with their first names. Rachel reached down and picked up her package. A small silver note fell to the ground. 'For your eyes only,' it read.

Rachel jumped as Sharav read the note over her shoulder. 'Sorry, had a little nap there. Feeling much better now.'

The three friends opened their packages and gazed at the most beautiful smart watches they had ever seen. Sharav gently lifted the watch out of the box and said, 'I think I am going to pee my pants!'

Each watch was made of solid stainless steel. They had round faces and felt very expensive. Paul placed the watch on his wrist and to his amazement the strap tightened itself. 'What! Did you see that?' he exclaimed.

'I wonder how you turn them on?' said Rachel, grinning as she placed the watch on her wrist. Instantly Rachel's watch turned itself on and a message on the face said, 'Checking DNA'.

'Oh, so you just say "on" and it turns on,' said Paul.

After ten seconds Rachel's watch announced in a French accent, 'DNA confirmed. Welcome to the IT watch, Rachel Fox, comment ça va? My name is Lucille.'

'Wow,' Paul said, stepping back. 'It talks!'

Sharav smiled broadly as his watch said, 'Hello Sharav, you can call me Arlo.'

'Paul, I'm freaking out here!' said Sharav.

Paul was laughing and getting acquainted with his watch, which was called Hugo.

'Paul,' said Hugo the watch, 'please wait for an

incoming message.'

Paul tilted his watch towards his face and suddenly a projected hologram of a friendly middle-aged man appeared a few feet in front of them. The man was smartly dressed, and he had a tanned face and grey hair, with deep lines near his mouth when he smiled.

'Good morning, you three,' said the hologram. 'Happy Christmas. I realise this is probably a little strange, but please bear with me. My name is William.'

Sharav leaned over to see where the face was coming from. He waved his hand towards the hologram and his hand passed through it. He looked at Paul's watch and saw that the hologram was projecting from the strap.

Paul managed to say 'Hi,' while staring open mouthed at the man in front of them. 'Can you see us?'

William laughed, 'Yes I can see you, there is a camera built into your watch. What is your watch called?' he smiled.

'Hugo, I think…' said Paul. 'We also have Arlo and Lucille.'

William smiled again. 'Interesting names. We let the watches pick their own names. Artificial intelligence is a wonderful thing. But just to reassure you, I am a real person and I'm speaking to you from London.'

Paul and Sharav looked at each other.

'Anyway, I realise that this is a bit odd. Sharav, would you mind pointing your watch towards your face so I can see you also? Great, thank you. My name is William and I work for a secret government agency called MI2. As you know, you have responded to the call to join us. I'm delighted with that. Thank you. I've heard great things about you all and we really could do with your help.'

'Do you not stop for Christmas?' asked Paul.

'We don't get great holidays here at MI2,' smiled William. 'Also, there are some operational pressures on the service currently that have required us to accelerate our recruitment process. The threat level has increased, so only a short Christmas lunch for us here at headquarters. Anyway, I know Natalie and Rob filled you in a bit about MI2.' The three of them nodded.

William continued, 'After your training you will

be asked to engage with operations where you will have to use your new knowledge and skills. We can guarantee excitement, hard work and at times, danger. However, we can monitor where and how you are through your new watches. Whether you join up or not is a very important decision and could alter the direction of your lives. Are you sure about this?'

Paul answered quickly, 'I'm sure. Happy to get started as soon as we can and get down to headquarters. Wherever that is.'

'Okay, great. Does everyone else agree?'

Sharav and Rachel nodded and smiled nervously.

'Good stuff. Okay, we are based in London. It's probably best that you use the cover story of joining the Army Cadet Force. We can supply all the paperwork. Any questions?'

The three of them shook their heads.

'Okay then, enjoy the rest of your Christmas and I'll hopefully see you soon.'

5

TAKEN

THE POLICE HAD visited Karen Fox a couple of times to gather information about Michael Fox and had filed a missing persons report. Karen had become quite distressed and had stopped sleeping, so Paul organised a visit from the GP who prescribed medication to help her sleep and to calm her anxiety.

Paul had spent most of Boxing Day and the day after pacing up and down his room desperate to get to London and help find his father. He was surprised that his mum agreed to them joining the Army Cadet Force. Mrs Fox had phoned Michael's brother, Stewart, to ask his opinion, and after the phone call she relented saying that it was probably good for them to keep occupied. Sharav had no problem getting permission from his parents, who agreed that a bit of adventure was always a good thing.

ON 29TH DECEMBER they were at Edinburgh Airport. They were asked to bring as little luggage as possible because everything they needed would be supplied at the MI2 headquarters. They expected to find themselves on an economy flight, however they boarded what looked like a private jet.

'Posh,' smiled Paul as he reached up to put his hand luggage in the overhead compartment.

The cabin was kitted out with eight expensive leather seats, four tables and high-quality HD televisions throughout.

After the flight checks were complete, the captain came back to speak to the three of them.

'Nice to meet you, Paul, Sharav and Rachel,' she smiled.

'Yes, good to meet you too,' said Paul. There was something about the pilot that made him feel uneasy.

'So, we're off to London?' the pilot inquired with a smile.

'Yes,' said Sharav, moving around in his seat. 'I hate flying. Do you have a lot of experience?'

'Yes,' laughed the pilot. 'You'll be perfectly safe. Okay, well, enjoy the flight, it will take about an hour and ten minutes to get there… if all goes to plan,' she said over her shoulder, as she returned to the cockpit.

Two minutes later a couple of men came onto the flight and with thick Eastern European accents, introduced themselves as Kevin and Jock. They kept the introductions short and sat near the front.

Shortly, after a quick safety demonstration from the air steward, they were in the air. They had been airborne for ten minutes when Paul's watch vibrated, prompting him to put in his headphones. Hugo greeted him saying, 'Paul, how are you today? My data tells me that Sharav has an increased heart rate and my measurements reveal an increased level of adrenaline. You might need to calm him down.'

Paul looked over at Sharav's red face and bulging eyes. 'That's pretty obvious,' he thought. 'Sharav, are you okay?'

'No, I'm not okay! We are 28,000 feet in the air. That is 5.3 miles above the ground in case you didn't know. The pilot looked like she wanted to kill me, there are two dodgy blokes sitting up front. And we are off to some crazy spy camp, which is ridiculous'.

Rachel and Paul looked at each other and smiled.

Hugo said, 'Let me gather some additional information to provide Sharav with some reassurance… checking…' Five seconds later the watch vibrated again.

'Paul, I don't want to alarm you, but I have some information which might be of use to you.'

Paul tried to stay calm as he waited for the news.

'It would appear that you have been led onto the wrong flight. You were due to leave on the R600 flight at 7.25 pm. However, you are on what would appear to be an unscheduled flight which left at 7.10 pm. My records tell me that this plane was sold by a Russian billionaire six months ago, to an unknown buyer from Algeria.' Paul's respiratory rate increased.

By this time Rachel was looking across at Paul, noticing the change in his demeanour. Hugo continued. 'I have alerted headquarters and will brief you once a plan has been formulated. In the meantime, please stay calm. It would appear you have a full bladder. I would suggest you visit the men's room. I find life is better with an empty bladder, wouldn't you agree?'

Paul dutifully visited the bathroom, keeping the news to himself.

On his return, Paul thought through all the possible scenarios. Who was that pilot? Those men seem tough. Were they flying to London? Could it be Algeria they were headed for?

His watch buzzed again, and he put in his headphones.

'Paul, hello,' said Hugo. 'Please direct your friends to put in their headphones.' Paul did so and soon they were all listening to the same message. It was William.

'Hello, you three,' William said cheerfully. 'So, I'm not sure if Paul has filled you in but it would appear that you are on the wrong flight. To put it bluntly, you have been abducted. It would seem that you are heading in the direction of South America. Perhaps to Colombia or Venezuela. You will soon be flying over Ireland and then across the Atlantic.

After the initial shock Paul smiled and said, 'Good one, William. Is this like one of those crazy initiation things?'

'Paul,' William said, 'I am deadly serious. This is real.'

6

THE FALL

PAUL, RACHEL AND Sharav looked at each other in disbelief.

Sharav said, 'But we haven't even been trained yet! I would at least have liked a "welcome to the club" speech before we have to deal with dangerous, crazy dudes who want us dead in Colombia!'

'Listen, Sharav,' said Paul, 'no one said anything about dying.'

Rachel nodded. 'Yep, Paul's right, there will be a way out of this.'

The air steward walked up the aisle and offered them a refreshment. She was taken aback when Paul declined. Sharav and Rachel asked for a soft drink. After the drinks had been served, Paul leaned forward and whispered, 'We can't take anything they offer us. They might want to drug us so we don't notice how long the flight is taking.'

Sharav pushed his glass to one side and sighed. 'This plan better be good!'

Just then, their watches buzzed in unison.

'Right you three, I convened the Lynx emergency committee. We have debated various rescue missions and have concluded that the scenario which provides us with the greatest chance of surv... success is Operation Kellner'.

Rachel interjected. 'Okay great, so how are you going to get the plane down safely? And does it involve fighter jets?'

'No, sorry,' said William. 'Scrambling jets is too high profile. We need literally to keep this under the radar.'

'Operation Kellner,' said Paul. 'I've heard that name before. Doesn't Kellner hold the Guinness world record for ...'

'Skydiving,' said William.

'OH, WAIT A MINUTE!' shouted Sharav, getting the attention of the two men at the front of the plane. He put his head in his hands and whispered, 'Tell me the plan doesn't involve skydiving'.

'Okay listen carefully,' said William. 'The plan involves skydiving. If these men are who we think they are, they will take you to South America and you won't be seen again. You need to get out of that plane before they exit UK and Irish airspace. Our options are limited after that. In forty minutes, you will be over the Atlantic Ocean. Currently you are ten minutes from Dublin. We have analysed the schematics of the plane you are in. It's a Legacy 500 and there is a storage cabin in the rear of the plane that holds five parachutes. We will be directing a commercial jet towards your plane, which should force the pilot to drop to 14,000 feet. This is a safer height for you to jump without oxygen.'

'I really hate heights,' whispered Sharav desperately. 'I really don't think I can do this!'

'Sharav, yes you can,' said William. 'You don't have a choice. Well you do have a choice but believe me, staying on the plane is the worse option.'

Paul was beginning to feel strangely exhilarated by the idea. He said, 'We need to know how to skydive.'

'Yes,' said William. 'And you don't have much time to learn. We are uploading a video to your phones. Please watch the five-minute video carefully. You then have seven minutes to locate the parachutes. I want you jumping out over Dublin if at all possible. We will soon have one of our agents in a helicopter. He will guide you down to the drop zone. The target is St Stephen's Green. Ever been there? It's lovely. Okay, watch the videos and remember your watches can help you.'

They spent the next five minutes frantically trying to focus on the tutorial video. The threat of jumping out of a plane in twelve minutes was an extremely effective learning aid. Once they had finished, Paul took a deep breath and casually walked to the rear of the plane to locate the parachutes. Rachel spent a couple of minutes trying to soothe Sharav. On his return, Paul said, 'Okay, found them. I've put the parachutes beside the toilet.'

Paul looked at Sharav, whose pupils were dilated, his head moving slowly from side to side.

'Sharav are you okay?' he asked.

'Oh yeah, I'm lovely,' Sharav said, slurring his speech and stroking the coat beside him. 'I mean, have you seen my cute chubby gerbil? I think my favourite animal would be a lovely, fluffy gerbil.'

Rachel's eyes widened with panic. 'Sharav, you seem drunk!' She darted a look at his glass and realised that half of the drink was gone.

'He drank the Coke!' she said, looking at Paul.

'Oh, what! We still need him to jump.'

'Gerbil, geerrrbilllll, hehe. I like to say gerrr-billllll. Bonk.' Sharav's limbs moved like they were made of rubber. He looked from one side of the plane to another and then giggled. 'I like this rainbow place. Oh, Paul… you are a unicorn. And your eyes…. They are soooo big and squishy. Can I squish your eyeballs?'

Paul stared at Sharav and then glanced at his watch, 'Okay we need to get him to the toilet, we only have five minutes.' Paul and Rachel pulled Sharav to his feet and guided him towards the back of the plane. The men at the front looked around questioningly and Paul shouted, 'He's not very well, we just need to visit the bathroom.' The men nodded and turned back in their seats. As they reached the toilet door Rachel let out a scream. Paul turned around quickly to see the larger of the two men with his hand on Rachel's shoulder.

'He okay, yes?' the man said with his thick accent.

'Yeah I think so,' said Paul.

'I use toilet before him, yes? I don't want him

make mess in toilet.'

'Oh, I don't know,' said Paul. 'He's really in a bad way, wouldn't want him puking over the leather seats in here would we?' Paul was desperate to get to the parachutes in the toilet before they were discovered.

Sharav laughed, 'I likey pukey, puke, puke... makes me laugh. Paul puke for me? Make me happy?' Sharav threw an inane smile toward the giant man. 'Do you likey puke? It's fun to lose your cookies?'

Something registered on the man's face and he said, 'I go first.' He pushed the three of them aside with one easy movement. Paul looked around frantically for a large object to hit him with. Before he could do anything, Rachel had taken her watch off and whispered, 'volts' into the microphone before throwing it at the man's back. The effect was instantaneous. He was thrown forward with such force that his body was hurled through the toilet door, taking it off its hinges, and his head smashed off the toilet. Just then, the plane took a nosedive and Rachel, Sharav and Paul lurched forward into the back of two leather seats. The plane was taking evasive action, in an attempt to avoid colliding with the commercial plane. Paul was holding onto Sharav to stop him slipping further down the plane away from their means of escape.

'Weeeeee,' squealed Sharav.

Paul shouted to Rachel. 'We've got to get those parachutes on. Only two minutes before the jump.' Rachel nodded as they started to clamber towards the toilet. The plane had begun to level off, which made the job of directing Sharav easier. 'I'm hungry, Paul,' Sharav said to him. 'Can you get me some jelly bellies?' He let out a cackle and said, 'Jeeellyyyy bellllieeeees.'

'Sorry pal, no jelly bellies tonight.'

Sharav frowned in his direction. Then he started crying, 'No jelly bellies. No sweeties for Shazza. No SWEETIES for Shazza, WAAA!'

'Shush,' said Paul. 'Listen I'll try to find you some jelly bellies. Just give me a minute.'

'Okay then,' grinned Sharav.

Rachel anxiously looked at her watch. 'We have one minute!'

They worked together to clip Sharav into his parachute and then quickly pulled their own packs on. As they finished, they saw the second man stride towards them. Paul pushed Rachel and Sharav towards the exit. He scanned the door and read, 'Danger. Do Not Touch.' 'Now or never,' he shouted. Then he reached for the handle, pulled it up and twisted. The air rushed into the plane and all three were sucked out into the night sky.

7

DUBLIN

PAUL, SHARAV AND Rachel found themselves in free fall over Dublin. Paul was tumbling uncontrollably with the light of the moon flashing in his eyes every half second. Finally, he managed to stabilise himself so he was falling stomach first. The sharp air cut through his thin jacket and he felt the discomfort of ice crystals forming in his nose. Then an anxious pain in his chest. Sharav. Paul looked to his right. He caught the white glint of Sharav's teeth as he tumbled through the air. Was he smiling? Paul remembered the video that told them to free fall for approximately 60 seconds before deploying the pilot chute. Paul looked at the altimeter on his watch. 10,000 feet. He knew he had to stop Sharav tumbling before the chute could be deployed.

'Come on Paul, focus... stay calm,' Paul thought to himself as he recalled the steps in deploying the parachute. To deploy the main chute, he had to pull the black handle on the lower right-hand side of his rig. If the main chute didn't work, the reserve chute could be released by pulling the white handle on the left-hand side. Paul took some comfort in knowing that there was an automatic activation device that would automatically deploy the parachute if they were still falling when they got to 1000 feet. Then it hit him. He got a horrible sick sensation in his stomach. None of them had turned on their automatic activation device. This was okay for him and Rachel, but Sharav was still drugged and there was no way he could pull any handle. Paul looked down at Dublin. The bright web of streets was racing towards them. He looked again at his watch, 5000 feet. This was the height they were due to break away from each other. He had to get to Sharav.

Paul leaned to his right. It was possible to manoeuvre in the air. He leaned further. The g-force wrenched him from his position and he hurtled towards Sharav, narrowly missing the top of his head. 'Okay,' thought Paul, 'small movements.' He leaned gradually left and found himself heading in Sharav's direction again, faster than he would like. Paul stretched out his arms and legs and managed to smash into his friend. He desperately grabbed onto his backpack. With a huge effort he moved Sharav onto his stomach. From the corner of his eye he saw a flash of an orange parachute shoot upwards. Rachel was safe. 'Where is that agent?' grunted Paul out loud. He glimpsed at his watch. 2400 feet. 'Should have deployed at 2500 feet,' thought Paul. Sharav was trying to turn around. He was trying to say something. He turned his head and gave Paul a huge grin. Paul's left hand lost his grip on Sharav and they were torn apart. 'NOOOOOOOOOOOO' shouted Paul. He looked at his watch again. 1500 feet. Paul knew that his last chance of saving both of them was to deploy at 1000ft. The distance between the friends was growing. Paul could feel his heartbeat through his entire body. He looked on, powerless to do anything.

'We need help,' shouted Paul.

Suddenly a green luminous object flashed past Paul and smashed into Sharav. Before Paul knew it, he had to lean left to avoid Sharav's parachute. With huge relief Paul pulled his own black handle and his parachute deployed.

The green luminous object turned out to be the agent. 'You're late!' shouted Paul, but his voice was lost in the rushing wind. All the energy suddenly drained from Paul. 'Got to concentrate,' Paul thought as he looked below towards the landing site. The agent's chute was bright green, so he was easy to follow towards the dark park below. Paul looked down on St Stephen's Green and he got a fright. The lake on the north side of the park narrowed in the middle and was divided by a bridge. It was as if he was being drawn towards two dark, monstrous eyes below.

Luckily it wasn't windy so Sharav continued to glide down towards the park. The agent was heading for the circular green section in the middle.

Paul followed the agent to the drop zone. As he got closer, he realised he was headed for the fountain. It was unavoidable. Paul's legs caught on the side of the fountain and he fell face down into the water. Rachel followed but landed perfectly on one of the sections of grass beside the 'keep off the grass' signs.

The agent unclipped his chute and walked towards them.

'How are we lads?' asked the agent in a strong

Dublin accent. 'I'm Conor, Conor O'Sullivan.' Conor looked about twenty years old. He was of medium build, six foot tall and had bright ginger hair. He had a friendly face that was covered in freckles.

'We are fine,' said Rachel. 'And we aren't both lads, I'm actually a girl'.

'Ah sure I can see that,' laughed Conor. 'You did well up there. Sure, you were absolutely fantastic.'

'Thanks,' said Paul, struggling to get the rig off his back.

Conor reached over saying, 'Sure look it, you unclip it here and there you go'. The pack slipped off Paul's back.

'Thanks,' said Paul, relieved to have rid himself of the pack and perhaps the trauma of the last ten minutes.

'You look a little white there, Paul,' said Conor. 'I'm thinking you might be experiencing a bit a shock. Need to get you some surgery tea.'

'Yea,' said Paul. The nausea grew in his stomach and there was an ache at the back of his head.

'Right so we better find your pal. Paul, you sit here while we go and get him. Actually here, eat this.' Conor reached into his pocket and pulled out a Mars bar and handed it to Paul. 'You'll be grand after that. Wait here'.

Paul sat on the edge of the fountain, glad to get some time on his own. He put his head between his legs and took some deep breaths. The park was deserted and the only noise he could hear was the nearby traffic.

Ten minutes later Conor, Rachel and a rather bedraggled looking Sharav returned. Rachel had linked arms with Sharav and was directing him towards the fountain.

'It was easy to find him,' said Rachel. 'These watches are amazing. We found him swinging in one of the trees quietly singing "Humpty Dumpty".'

'Nothing wrong with a bit a Humpty Dumpty,' smiled Conor.

Sharav burst out laughing, pointing at Conor and putting on an Irish accent, 'to be sure.... a bit a Humpty Dumpty.'

Rachel looked at Paul. 'It would seem that there is nothing funnier than Conor's accent.' She guided Sharav to sit beside Paul. Paul put his arm behind him to ensure he didn't lose his balance and fall into the water.

'Isn't this lovely now,' said Conor looking around St Stephen's Green. 'Lot a history here, you know. I love a bit a history, let me tell you a bit. So, during the Easter Rising of 1916 about 250 insurgents set up in St Stephen's Green. They nicked some motor vehicles to set up roadblocks around the park. But in the end, it wasn't so clever. The British Army just walked into the Shelbourne Hotel over there, went up to the top floor and started shooting down at them. So, they had to leg it. Stupid really.'

Paul, Rachel and Sharav looked at him open mouthed as he told them the story. When he finished, Sharav burst out laughing again, 'they had to leg it, ha ha ha ha.'

Rachel said, 'Fascinating, Conor, but do you think we could get out of here?'

'Ah no problem. Just one more thing.' Conor was bursting to tell them another fact. 'During the Easter Rising they had a ceasefire, so the park rangers could feed the ducks! Good old Irish, know how to look after their ducks.'

'Der ducks!' giggled Sharav. 'Der ducks! To be sure.... how's the craic...... Janey Mac. She's got a face on her like a plate of mortal sins!' Sharav fell forward and was rolling around on the gravel.

Conor laughed, 'Right, let's go. We are going out the north gate and off to the safe house in Pearse Square. It's about a 25-minute walk.'

8

JACKS

As THEY EXITED St Stephen's Green they turned right. Soon they were walking up Kildare Street, surrounded by a mix of modern and historic buildings. Conor pointed out the National Museum of Ireland telling them some of the history of the building, which Paul promptly forgot. Rachel looked interested though and asked some polite questions.

As they were walking up the street, Conor pointed out Leinster House. It was an impressive house with four huge columns and a lot of windows. Conor said, 'So that is Leinster House. It was originally called Kildare House after the Earl of Kildare, who had it built....' Paul didn't hear the rest of the three-minute history lesson.

'Fascinating, isn't it!' said Conor enthusiastically.

'Wow,' said Paul unconvincingly.

Rachel shot Paul a look and her eyes widened, as

if to say, 'stay interested!'

'Anyway, we might need to go to that gaff tomorrow,' said Conor. 'I need to introduce you to someone.'

Paul was confused but didn't pursue it any further.

By this point Sharav was beginning to come around. He shook his head and looked at his surroundings. 'Where are we?'

Paul smiled and said, 'Welcome back, Sharav. We are in Dublin and you, my friend, have been as high as a kite for over an hour.'

Rachel cut in. 'Sharav, remember that Coke on the plane?'

'Yeah.'

'You drank it, didn't you?'

'You know I can't resist Coke.'

'Well, it turns out that you were drugged. Luckily neither Paul nor I took a drink, so we were able to get you out of the plane.'

Things started to become clear to Sharav. 'You mean we jumped out the plane?'

'Yep,' smiled Paul. 'With a parachute…. and you nearly died! It was stressful. I tried to save your life.

But in the end, it was Conor here who turned up to save the day. Late, mind you!'

Sharav looked at Conor and said, 'Eh thanks, so you are the agent we were told about?'

'That's right, good to meet you. Welcome to Dublin. I've just been telling your friends about the fascinating history of these buildings. Actually, I have something else to say…'

Paul interrupted. 'Thanks very much, Conor, but maybe later. I am desperate for a pee.'

'Ah yeah. You need to go to the jacks for a slash? Sure, that's fine.'

'I don't think so,' replied Paul. 'Just a toilet will be fine.'

Conor laughed, 'Ah sorry. The jacks. That's what I mean. Jacks is a word we use for toilet over here. And if you want a good old-fashioned toilet, I have just the place for you. It's at the end of this street.'

They all walked to the end of Kildare Street and then turned right onto Leinster Street. There were some high railings that led onto a park. Conor told them that it was College Park and that it backed onto Trinity College. He pointed out a gap in the railings just across the road and said, 'There's an underground toilet just over there.'

Sharav started to say, 'Yeah I could do with…,' but then he stopped when he saw the dark place where Conor was pointing. 'Actually, it's fine. I'll hold on.'

'We'll wait here,' said Conor.

Paul crossed the road. He looked at his watch. It was 9 pm. He approached the entrance and saw that the walls leading down to the toilet were covered with white and blue tiles. As he was walking slowly down the steps the smell of urine was overpowering. There was some rubbish on the bottom step and the light leading into the main area was flickering on and off. As he descended the stairs, Paul had second thoughts, but he was so desperate that he kept going. It was a large space with about 10 urinals on the far wall and three cubicles nearest him. The light went off for two seconds and then came on again. Paul ran for a cubicle and quickly locked the door behind him. He started humming to himself to calm the fear. Then he heard a noise. He stopped breathing and listened. Nothing. He flushed the toilet and turned to open the door. As he opened the door, he was relieved to see that there was no one else there. The light went out again. Paul froze, waiting for the light to come on. Time stood still. The bulb flickered on briefly and Paul let out a shout. There in front of him was a mountain of a man who was as wide as he was tall. Maybe it was just his imagination. The light came on again, this time for longer. No, this was real. There in front of Paul with a sickening smile on his face, was a man with a large shaved head, black stubble, and dark eyes that were close together. Paul backed away into the toilet. The man grabbed Paul by the scruff and dragged him out into the open area. He flung him across the floor like a doll. Paul skidded on his back and hit his head off the far wall. He pushed back with his legs trying to move away from the man who was striding towards him. Paul was lifted up into the air with such ease that he knew he was in real trouble. Then he remembered his watch. He didn't have time to say anything before he was flung across the room again. He managed to put his hands in front of his head to reduce the impact against the tiled wall. He put his hand to his chest gasping for air.

'Hugo…' Paul managed to get out.

'Yes, Paul? You seem a little out of breath. Heart

is racing too.'

'I need…' Paul looked up to see the man towering over him, '…help.' As quick as he could, he turned the watch face so that Hugo could see the man.

'Paul, I see you are in great danger. Please wait. Help is on the way.'

THE OTHER THREE were having a pleasant conversation outside. They were laughing as Rachel explained to Sharav how funny he had found Conor's Irish accent when he was still a little high on whatever drug had been in his Coke. Conor's phone buzzed. He glanced at it. 'Code red. Paul in serious danger.' Before Rachel and Sharav had a chance to ask what was wrong, they saw Conor sprint across the road towards the underground toilet. A car screeched to a halt as Conor leapt over the bonnet.

9

THE FIGHT

MEANWHILE THE MAN had Paul by the scruff again and lifted him up to his eye level. 'Are you Paul Fox?' he grunted.

Paul breathed heavily and then said, 'Yeah and who are you?'

'You're coming with me. We need to organise a little family reunion.'

Just then Conor appeared and looked at them both. 'Howaya lads. Looks like you're having some fun.'

Paul landed in a heap on the floor. He crawled towards the urinals and wiped blood from his forehead. The man turned to Conor and looked him up and down. Paul didn't fancy Conor's chances against this huge gorilla of a man.

'Not your party. Leave now and you won't get hurt,' said the man.

'Eh, can't do that. Sorry.'

The man pulled a knife from his belt, smiled and walked towards Conor slowly.

'Ah sure there is no need for that.' said Conor. 'Paul, you okay? This might be a good opportunity for you to get your first lesson in self-defence. I'll talk you through it.'

Rachel and Sharav appeared on the bottom step and Conor looked at them. 'Okay, you two stay where you are. Everything's going to be fine. First things first. He's got a knife which isn't great, so we have to disarm him. Number of options here. I'll go for the slap.'

Conor quickly slapped the back of the man's hand with an upwards motion and the knife flew across the room, rattling against the far wall.

The man looked confused and then angry.

Conor continued. 'Best to keep it simple, you see if you hit the knuckles hard enough, the assailant will release the knife. So, let's say I kick him with me left leg.' Conor aimed a kick at his ribs and the man grabbed hold of his leg. 'And if he catches it, like so, then I can spin around and hit him with the heel of me right foot.' Conor leapt into the air, spun around and landed a kick to the man's head. The man fell to the floor slightly dazed and they both stood up again.

'So,' said Conor. 'When you feel ready, Paul, please stand up and start edging your way around to the exit. We'll be finished here shortly. Normally I try to keep these interactions short, but I'll show you a couple of more things.'

Conor ran at the man with his head down and was promptly grabbed in a head lock. Conor pushed him with his shoulders, grabbed the man's huge legs and lifted them upwards. This sent him crashing onto his back.

'That was called the double leg take down. Effective, don't you think? It's getting late and I can see you are all hungry, so let's finish. Couple of options here, I could try the 540 tornado kick, which is impressive but not something you'll be able to do right away. So instead I think I'll try the wall jump.' The man was shaking his head as he got up. His face was bright red and he let out an almighty roar.

'You are going to pay!' he shouted as he ran towards Conor. With the grace and power of a gymnast, Conor ran towards the far wall, jumped and pushed himself off the top a urinal and bounced off the side wall before doing a 360 spinning kick, catching the man hard on the head and knocking him out cold. Conor landed. 'Ta da!' he smiled, giving a small bow.

Sharav and Rachel found themselves clapping. 'Just like the movies,' said Sharav in wonder.

'Let's get some food,' said Conor, helping Paul towards the stairs. Rachel took hold of Paul's other arm and pushed some of his hair out of the way to look at his head wound. She dabbed it with a tissue and told Paul to press firmly in order to stem the blood. As they came out into the open, they saw the familiar golden arches and headed towards them.

ONCE THEY HAD eaten something, Sharav turned to Conor and said, 'Listen Conor, you seem a nice person and everything. Please can you explain a few things to us. So, we signed up to this a few days ago. We are supposed to be on our way to headquarters in London and already we've been abducted, nearly died falling out of an aeroplane and Paul here almost had his face smashed in by that gorilla man. I'm kinda thinking we have made a terrible mistake. Plus, we are in Dublin and not London! Help us out here.'

'Ah sure you're grand,' said Conor. 'I don't actually know that much. I got a call a couple of hours ago to do a heli jump and wasn't told all the details. All I know is that you three were on your way to London and needed some help because some eejits kidnapped you all. It's been good craic so far, hasn't it?'

'No,' said Rachel. 'It hasn't. Who do you work for?'

'Ah well, yeah, you see the British and the Irish have a collaboration agreement between their different spy agencies. We share intelligence and help each other out. I'm 21 and for six years I've been working for G2, which is basically the Irish Intelligence Agency.'

'You seem very laid back about all this,' said Rachel.

'Well I'm getting used to it all. I've seen quite a lot of stuff, you know. And I suppose the secret to staying relaxed is regular Hail Marys and me mammy's cooking. I don't actually live with her anymore. I share a flat with a few pals, but I go home for grub as often as possible'.

Paul started getting flashbacks of the attack in the underground toilet and looked straight at Conor.

'That man knew my name!'

'Did he?' said Conor.

'Yeah, he said, "Are you Paul Fox?" He said something about a family reunion. How can a random bloke in Dublin know who I am?'

'Hmmm,' Conor rubbed his chin. 'He wasn't a random bloke. I've seen his kind before. My guess is that he was hired to abduct you.'

Paul thought back to the message in the £2 coin, 'There are dangerous people who will try to stop you at all costs.' The reality of that message was starting to sink in.

'Anyway,' said Conor. 'I have to get you to the safe house and then to London. Maybe you'll find out more when you get there?'

'Suppose,' said Paul, who was still feeling overwhelmed. Rachel put her hand on his back and gave him a pat, saying, 'Let's just wait and see what they say at headquarters.'

TEN MINUTES LATER the group arrived at Pearse Square. It was a well-kept square with gardens in the centre, the length of a football pitch. Conor smiled and told them that it was a Georgian garden square which dated back to 1893. They climbed a number of steps up to the door of 46 Pearse Square Gardens. It was a brown brick, terraced house with ivy climbing up the walls on either side of a red door. Conor opened the door and stood to the side. 'Welcome to the safe house,' he grinned, and the three adventurers trudged in.

10

LEINSTER HOUSE

PAUL WOKE UP and lay still for a minute, trying to remember where he was and how he got there. He squinted towards the window as the sunlight streamed into the room through the pale pink curtains. Then he remembered where he was. The safe house. His second thought was for his dad. 'We've got to get to London,' he said quietly. He glanced at his watch, 11 am.

Paul looked at his surroundings. Half of the laminate floor was covered in cardboard and the walls had wood panelling up to chest height. The upper section was covered in faded clown patterned wallpaper that made him shiver. He stood up and immediately felt lightheaded as he limped towards the window.

Paul pulled back the translucent curtain and looked out onto Pearse Square. The gardens looked beautiful in the morning light. Paul saw a couple of people walking towards the central area of the gardens. A large light green statue rose up from the central flower bed. Paul looked more closely at the figures walking in the garden and realised that it was Conor and Sharav. They appeared to be engrossed in deep conversation. Sharav's shoulders were raised and his walk was stilted. Conor wasn't walking with his relaxed swagger. 'That's odd,' thought Paul.

Paul got dressed and, with a rumble of his stomach, walked through to the kitchen. The smell of damp filled his nostrils as he walked across the orange tiled floor. He looked through all the cupboards and found a few tea bags. He put the kettle on.

'Morning, Paul,' said Rachel, as she came in through the kitchen door carrying two bags. 'I've got some breakfast. Hungry?' Rachel had always been a morning person.

'Hi. Yes please, I'm starving.'

Rachel was followed by Sharav and then Conor.

'Morning,' they said in unison.

'How are we this morning?' asked Conor, looking at Paul.

'Yeah good, thanks. I slept for ages. Must have been knackered.'

'Good, glad you slept well.'

'You go out for a walk?' asked Paul.

'Yeah, Sharav and me went out to explore the square. The sun is gorgeous this morning. Lovely.'

'Right,' said Paul, who wondered why Sharav seemed distracted.

Sharav and Rachel prepared a breakfast of corn-flakes, warm, buttered toast and cups of tea. After which, Rachel threw a bag of marshmallows into the middle of the table. 'Conor told me to spend as much as I wanted,' she smiled.

Conor explained the plan for the day. 'Right so, I'm hoping today will be a little bit more relaxed than yesterday. I want you to meet my boss, Mary O'Connell. She's at Leinster House. Do you remember it from yesterday?' Everyone nodded. 'Well, we'll go there today and chat with me boss about how to get you to London. Sound like a plan?'

'Sounds good,' said Sharav. 'I love old buildings.'

'Yeah, it's beautiful in there. The economy might be on its knees, but Leinster House reminds us of better days. Okay, let's get packed up and we'll head over there now.'

THIRTY MINUTES LATER the group were walking down Kildare Street. Rachel, Sharav and Paul had really warmed to Conor in the short time that they'd known him. Conor proudly pointed out that this was Ireland's most prestigious street and boasted some extraordinary buildings that were steeped in Irish history. They finally turned towards Leinster House. The largest Georgian mansion in Dublin stood proud in the winter sunlight.

'It looks like a palace in the daylight,' gasped Rachel.

'Yeah, I love this place,' smiled Conor. 'I don't get to come to this gaff very much, so we are lucky that the boss is here today. Security isn't as tight today cause the Parliament isn't sitting.'

As they walked through the huge wooden door of Leinster House they were surrounded by warm light. They spent time studying the intricate archways on either side of the hall. They all stood in the large, square hall and looked up to take in the beautiful Waterford crystal chandelier and breath-taking ceiling which appeared to have been painted in pure gold.

'Look over here,' said Conor as he proudly showed them the proclamation of Ireland's independence and the various portraits of Irish leaders including Eamon de Valera and Michael Collins.

They were led down a number of grand corridors, floored in plush blue carpet. Sharav was at the back of the line and was so impressed by the bounce of the carpet that he started doing a funny trampoline walk. They finally came to a room that the plaque outside declared was the 'Ceremonial Garden Room'. Conor knocked on the door and they heard a simple, 'Come' from the other side. They entered a bright room with deep blue and yellow walls. Photos of past visitors to Leinster House adorned the walls, including three American presidents which Sharav noticed straight away: JFK, Ronald Reagan and Bill Clinton. A woman approached them with an easy, relaxed manner. Mary O'Connell stood tall, her long white hair was tied back, and her piercing blue eyes showed insight and intelligence.

'This is Mary O'Connell,' Conor announced, and then introduced them all as if he had known them for years. Paul noticed that Mary spent a long time shaking his hand. And there was something in her eyes which left him feeling that Mary knew more about him than she was letting on.

'You look just like...' Mary's sentence tailed off. 'Anyway, it's great to meet you all. I believe you are new recruits of MI2 and the last 48 hours have been—'

'Terrible,' interjected Rachel. 'It wasn't really what we were expecting.'

'I'm sure it wasn't!' agreed Mary. 'Listen, I asked Conor to bring you here so we can plan how best to get you to London safely. Given the events so far, I want to take extra care of you all. I've spoken to William in your London Headquarters and we feel it would be better that you travel by car and boat, rather than risk another flight.'

'Hallelujah!' smiled Sharav.

'We really need to get there as soon as possible,' said Paul, looking at Mary.

'Yes Paul, of course. The ferry may take a bit longer, but your safety is our priority. Conor, we think it is best you get out of Dublin and take the Rosslare to Plymouth ferry. It leaves at 9:15 this evening and takes about nine hours. You will be sailing on the *Oscar Wilde* ship. Oh, and Conor, I think you should bring Darragh with you.'

Conor hesitated but quickly recovered and said, 'Ah sure, the more the merrier.'

'He's actually sitting behind that sofa over there.'

Rachel, Paul and Sharav looked towards the dark blue sofa waiting for someone to appear. Conor walked around the back of the sofa and looked down saying, 'Howaya Darragh?' There was a silent pause, and he said, 'Ah good, I'm glad. Been up to much...no? Ah well. Sure, you can come and help me get these three to London. Sound good? Great.'

Paul looked at Sharav and began to think Conor had lost his mind. They all edged slowly towards the sofa and finally peeked far enough around to see a small thin figure, crouched behind the sofa eating a packet of green M&Ms. Darragh suddenly jumped up and eyed them suspiciously. The group leaned back staring at the young person who had dark hair, small eyes and a pointy face. Darragh was shorter than them all and looked so thin and undernourished. He was dressed in black from his trainers right up to his baseball cap.

Conor registered the alarm on all their faces. 'This

is Darragh. Darragh Lemon.'

At the mention of 'Lemon,' Darragh furtively scanned all their faces looking for any sign of amusement. He was extremely sensitive about his size and his surname. Conor continued, 'Darragh is our secret weapon. He might be small, but he is extremely fierce and one of the best agents we've got.'

Mary walked over to the group. 'I want to make sure you get to London without any further complications, which is why I am asking Conor and Darragh to accompany you on your travels. Conor, you'll need a car to get to Rosslare and then to London on the other side. Feel free to take any of the cars from the basement.'

Conor looked at his three new friends with a delighted grin on his face. 'Wait until you see the basement!'

11

ROAD TRIP

'PAUL AND RACHEL, can I catch you for a minute?' asked Mary, glancing briefly at Conor.

'Let's step outside,' said Conor, shepherding Sharav and Darragh through the door.

'It's great to meet you both,' said Mary when they were alone. 'Have a seat. I heard that your father has gone missing.'

'How did you...?' began Paul.

'I get to know things,' smiled Mary, waving away his question. 'Anyway, I have some information that might be useful in your quest to find your father. I had a couple of our analysts do some digging and they have confirmed the suspicion that there is an active mole within MI2.'

'Yes, we heard that too!' said Paul.

'We have reason to believe that the mole's code-name is Sabre.'

'Sabre?'

'Yes, and as the newest recruits you have a unique opportunity to uncover the mole. My advice is to learn quickly and be very careful whom you trust. If you need any help, please don't hesitate to contact me, or indeed Conor.'

'How do we know we can trust you?'

'You don't,' smiled Mary. 'Welcome to the world of espionage! Now go and choose a car.'

FIVE MINUTES LATER Paul, Rachel and Sharav found themselves entering a lift with Conor and Darragh. The door of the lift had been concealed behind a full-length, ornate mirror at the end of one of the corridors. Paul saw that Rachel was keeping her eye on Darragh. Darragh moved in an unpredictable fashion and had a crazy look in his eye. Darragh continued to eat green M&Ms as the lift descended into the basement. As they exited the lift Conor grinned at them, as if all his Christmases had come at once. The three young people were treated to a spectacular view of metallic, shiny goodness. Set before them was a basement full of high-end sports cars. Each of the sixteen cars was a different model and colour. Rachel was first to walk towards them; her mouth was open as she gazed at each one in turn.

'You are having a laugh!' she exclaimed. She walked towards the nearest car which was a deep red with two white stripes on the bonnet. 'A 2010 Ford Shelby CT500! 0-60 in 4.6 seconds. A 2011 Aston Martin DB9. 470 brake horsepower and costs £122,445 brand new!'

Sharav shook his head and said, 'Rachel, I didn't know you were into cars!'

Paul followed Rachel and smiled, saying, 'It's funny, it was like she was born loving cars. Exactly like Dad.'

Rachel continued, 'Oh an Audi A8, a Lamborghini Huracán and a beautiful, gold Bentley Bentayga. She approached a black, space-age looking car. 'Oh, my goodness, a Lamborghini Reventon! 0-60 in 3.3 seconds, maximum speed 211mph, 8000 RPM and costs over a million pounds! Is this real? Don't wake me up if it's a dream.'

Conor, also impressed by Rachel's car knowledge, smiled and said, 'Yep, and we can choose any car we want!'

Sharav looked confused. 'I thought spies were

supposed to keep a low profile!'

'Not in Ireland!' laughed Conor.

Rachel looked at Conor and said, 'Well, the Lamborghini won't seat us all. How about the Ford Shelby? Please can we have that one?' Conor shook his head.

'Okay,' said Rachel as she looked around her again. 'What about the Aston Martin? Loads of space for us all. Or the Bentley?'

Conor shook his head again. 'Nope, you still haven't mentioned me favourite car.'

Rachel pointed at the silver Audi.

'No,' said Conor. 'Come over here.'

Conor walked over to the far wall of the basement. He turned to face the group and pointed at what looked like an empty parking space. They walked up to him and there, hiding behind the Bentley, was a red Mini with white stripes.

Rachel looked aghast. 'Oh, come on! Not the 1963 Mini Cooper! I'll settle for the BMW M2.'

'1963 Mini Cooper S,' corrected Conor. 'With modifications. This is by far me favourite car out of all the other cars here. I've driven each one of them and we will have way more fun in this. It's got a

1071cc engine, a vacuum assisted brake booster and a second fuel tank fitted. Oh, and some other surprises. This little beauty won the Monte Carlo Rally in 1964, 1965 and 1967.'

'But it's 56 years old and it's only got 4 seats!' Rachel was almost shouting at this point.

'Ah, but Darragh is happy to sit in the middle.'

Darragh gave them a grin, revealing a mouth of grey and black teeth, four of which were missing. Sharav took an involuntary step backwards. Darragh, realising he had let his guard down, quickly covered his mouth with his hand and glared at them all. Each person quickly looked away, pretending they were interested in one of the cars.

IT WASN'T LONG before they were all on the road, Conor happily in the driver's seat, fiddling with the ancient radio trying to find some music. Paul was in the passenger seat up front and Darragh was sandwiched between Rachel and Sharav in the back.

Conor piped up. 'Darragh, show them your M&M trick.' Darragh glowered at Conor and then at everyone else. He paused, looked at his bag of M&Ms and very slowly reached his left hand down to pick one out. Everyone apart from Conor was transfixed as Darragh balanced the single M&M on the tip of his little finger. He was totally focused as he slowly moved the M&M towards his nose. He went cross-eyed. They all held their breath as they waited to see what would happen next. Darragh moved his finger with the M&M slowly away from his nose and readied himself. He moved his right hand up to the M&M and readied himself to flick it. But just before flicking the M&M he turned his head slowly towards Sharav, staring at him with wide eyes and an open mouth. Sharav looked back, holding his breath with his eyebrows raised. It all happened so fast. Darragh flicked the M&M hard. The M&M flew past Paul's left ear, bouncing off his side window, the front windscreen, Rachel's side window and finally hitting Sharav hard on the head before bouncing into Darragh's mouth. Conor cheered as Darragh sat back in his seat, crunching the sweet with a satisfied look on his face.

They were now out of Dublin and making good progress along the M11. The sun was shining again, and they were all enjoying the scenery as they passed the Wicklow mountains.

Thirty minutes into their trip Darragh looked behind them and tapped Conor on the shoulder. 'Tail,' he said in a very broad Dublin accent.

Conor looked in his mirror. 'You sure?'

'Yeah,' Darragh replied, whilst digging into his M&M bag again.

Conor changed lanes and slowed down a little. 'Looks like we might have company, everyone. It's not a problem, we can easily lose them if needed. Please don't look back cause you'll alert them that we've blown their cover.' Paul looked into the side mirror and spotted a dark blue Ford Mondeo two cars behind them.

Conor signalled to turn off at the next exit. The Ford Mondeo did the same. But at the last-minute Conor pulled back on the main road. So did the other car.

'Okay, so we definitely do have a tail. Darragh, we need a plan.'

'Enniscorthy,' said Darragh, totally relaxed.

'Hmm, good idea. Lots of narrow, windy streets that we can lose them on.' Conor put his foot on the accelerator and the Mini sped up. As they were taking the turn-off for Enniscorthy, Conor became aware of a blue flashing light behind them. 'Ah Janey Mac, it's not a tail, it's the police! Better pull over.' Conor pulled onto the hard shoulder. The Ford Mondeo drove up behind them and two plain-clothes men got out of the car. They stayed near their own car, talking into a radio.

Conor reassured the group, 'Don't worry everyone, once they realise the car is registered to G2 things will be fine.'

Darragh looked behind him again and simply said, 'Not the Garda.'

'What! Really? They're not the police?' Conor said, sounding worried.

Paul spoke into his watch. 'Hugo, check a registration for me, will you? It's 12-D-36472.'

'Just checking, Paul, please wait.'

Meanwhile both the men were approaching the Mini. Darragh said again, 'Not the Garda.'

'Hugo, quickly please.' Both the men had reached the back of the Mini when Paul's watch said, 'This blue Ford Mondeo was registered stolen 24 hours ago.'

Conor frantically grabbed and turned the ignition key. He threw the gear stick into first and put his foot to the floor.

The Mini sped away from the two men. Conor saw in his rear-view mirror one man pull a gun from his belt. Conor shouted, 'GET DOWN, EVERYONE!' Everyone ducked apart from Darragh, who sat bolt upright chewing happily. The bullet hit the back of the car, luckily missing the rear left tyre. Sharav's head slumped forward. He was asleep again.

'Okay,' said Conor, 'now you'll see what this Mini is made of!'

12

ENNISCORTHY

CONOR SPED TOWARDS the town centre. Paul and Rachel looked behind them, frantically checking where the gunmen were.

'Wow this little car can really move!' laughed Paul as the Mini pulled away from the Mondeo.

'Can anyone smell petrol?' asked Rachel.

'Oh yeah,' said Conor sniffing. 'They must have hit the petrol tank. Looks like we are losing fuel.'

Sharav woke up. 'Anyone hurt?'

'No, but we are losing some fuel,' replied Rachel.

Conor reassured them by saying, 'It's okay, remember I said we had another fuel tank. It's LPG so it should be fine… unless…' his voice trailed off.

'Unless what?' Sharav asked.

'Gun,' said Darragh staring into Sharav's face. 'Gun, Gun, Gun!'

'What he means is, if they shoot the LPG tank

things might get nasty.'

Rachel piped up, 'LPG stands for Liquid Petroleum Gas and it's highly flammable. It's fine if there is no oxygen in the tank but the bullet would definitely cause an explosion.'

'BOOM!' shouted Darragh, making Sharav scream.

'Lord help us!' exclaimed Sharav. 'Conor, get us out of here!'

Paul was enjoying the rush of adrenaline and he smiled broadly. 'Have you done your terrorist evasion driving course?'

'Nope! Doing it next month though,' said Conor.

Suddenly Conor pulled on the handbrake, turned the car left and managed to squeeze the Mini through a gap in a stone wall that led through a park. They sped down the short path past a man and his dog. The dog gave a sharp yelp as he was tugged away from the oncoming vehicle. They heard a series of expletives as the man shook his fist at the Mini, which then bumped down a kerb back onto the road. The Mini skidded round a U-shape bend. Many of the mid-morning shoppers stood still, staring at the Mini filled with people. The Ford was nowhere to be seen.

'Oh, praise the Lord,' said Sharav, leaning back into his seat.

As they approached the centre of the town they came to a fork in the road. There was a large, yellow hotel at the intersection, with a seating area where some of Enniscorthy's residents were enjoying the morning sun. Conor took the left-hand fork and put his foot down.

Darragh mumbled, 'Should have gone right.' Within two seconds the Ford Mondeo came speeding down from a road on their left and screeched to a halt in front of them. Conor slammed on the brakes. Darragh wasn't wearing a seat belt so he was cata-pulted into the front of the car and ending up lying on his back between Paul and Conor. Darragh, still clutching his M&M bag, grinned up at Paul. Conor pushed Darragh closer to Paul so he could reach the gear stick.

One of the men wound down his window and pointed a gun towards the Mini.

Sharav shouted, 'NO BOOM PLEASE, NO BOOM!' And fell asleep again.

Conor threw the gear stick into first and turned

right. The Mini bounced up the kerb between two huge steel bollards and onto the pedestrian area. A couple of people had to jump out of the way as the Mini zigzagged between the bins, trees and benches. As they approached the four huge steps leading down onto the other road, Conor sped up. The men in the other car watched helplessly as the Mini flew through the air and landed hard on the road below. The Mondeo was too wide to follow. Its tyres screeched as they accelerated, looking for a right turn.

Meanwhile Conor took a sharp right and sped the wrong way down a narrow one-way street.

Suddenly Darragh growled, 'Only two left!' as he looked into the M&M bag. For the first time since meeting him, Paul saw fear in Conor's eyes.

'Okay,' said Conor. 'We can't let him run out of M&Ms. Paul grab the bag.' Darragh clasped the bag close to his chest and quickly looked from Conor to Paul and back again. He bared his black teeth and growled at Paul.

'What! I can't take them off him!' said Paul. 'Are you mad?'

'I don't have time to explain Paul, but you have to get that bag off him, or we are in serious trouble.'

Paul hesitated and then grabbed for the bag. Darragh held on with a vice-like grip and let out an angry 'Miiiiiiiinnnnnne!' Paul pulled hard and almost succeeded when Darragh with lightning speed sunk his teeth into Paul's leg.

'Ahhhhhhhhhhhh! He bit my leg! He bit me!'

Rachel looked on in alarm, helpless to do anything apart from try to hold Darragh's flailing legs still.

Conor pulled the handbrake on and spun the car 180 degrees. The Mini swung around and stopped perfectly in a disabled car parking space behind a wall.

'Darragh!' he said angrily. 'You can't bite people!'

'My M&Ms!' Darragh shouted.

'Okay listen, we have to get him more M&Ms or he will literally tear this car apart.' He thrust his hand into his pocket and pulled out twenty Euro. Opening his car door, he got out and looked into the back seat.

'Rachel, can you please go and buy some M&Ms? Buy all you can get with twenty Euro. I'm sure I saw a corner shop just up the street a bit. Those men would recognise me but probably not you.'

Rachel looked astonished. 'Conor, we are being

chased by armed men! Do we really have time to stop for sweets?'

Conor noticed Sharav was asleep and raised an eyebrow. He sighed, 'Listen I know it isn't ideal, but I've seen what happens when Darragh runs out of M&Ms. He loses it. Please trust me, we have got to get those sweets.'

Rachel nodded and took the money. 'I'll be back in a minute.' Conor had his hand on the ignition key as they waited. Rachel finally returned with an armful of M&Ms, 'They aren't all green, but it was the best I could get.'

Sharav was awake again and Darragh was upright in the back seat. Rachel handed over the sweets and Darragh gathered the bags into his arms like they were precious little chicks.

'Right so!' said Conor brightly. 'Things are looking up. Sure, let's get outta here.'

Conor drove the Mini more slowly now as there was no sign of their pursuers. Darragh contentedly ate his sweets, although he sometimes threw a suspicious look at Rachel and Sharav, holding the sweets closer to his chest.

Suddenly, the blue Ford smashed into the back of

the Mini, sending it into a spin. The Mini spun through revolutions. Conor hit his head on the window and when they came to a halt he was dazed and confused. The men got out of the Ford and approached the Mini from behind, pointing their guns towards the gas tank. Paul shouted, 'Conor reverse!' Conor was shaking his head struggling to focus.

Paul thrust his right leg over the gear stick pushing down hard on top of Conor's foot onto the clutch. He pulled the gear stick to the left and then up and shouted 'accelerate!'

Conor slammed the accelerator down to the floor and crashed into both men, knocking them over. The Mini's tyres smoked as it sped off. Sharav looked back to see the men slowly get back up again and one of them limped towards the car. 'They aren't dead!' said Sharav, relieved.

Conor was steering from right to left, narrowly missing cars and hitting the kerb a couple of times.

'Conor, pull over,' said Rachel. 'I'll drive.'

Conor sat in the back and Rachel took over, grinning broadly as she did so.

As they passed some shops Darragh piped up,

'Into Dunnes.'

Rachel threw the car left into a three-story car park which would give them excellent cover. The Mini quickly made its way up each story until they came to a stop sign, 'Warning: building in progress.'

Rachel got out of the Mini and pulled the temporary barrier to one side. Soon they were on the roof of the car park. 'No safety barriers! Anyone could fall off the edge of this building,' Sharav exclaimed, as everyone apart from Darragh got out of the car to have a look around.

Ten minutes later, Conor was talking into his watch. Sharav was a safe five metres away from the edge, whilst Paul was enthusiastically re-living the car chase with Rachel. They were all basking in the relief of their escape when out of the corner of his eye Paul saw a flash of blue. He stepped closer to the edge of the flat roof to have a better look. Sharav and Rachel watched Paul turn quickly and stride towards Conor who was now sitting on the bonnet of the Mini. 'Conor, the men are back. We're trapped!'

13

WET

'EVERYONE IN!' SHOUTED Conor. Rachel, Sharav and Paul jumped into the Mini.

Conor lifted his wrist and spoke into his watch, 'Bryan, we're trapped. Please advise on escape options. I'm thinking there might only be one option, but I'd like to avoid it if possible.'

'Of course, Conor, please wait.' Just a few seconds later Conor's watch spoke again, 'Conor, you are correct, there is only one way out. Please see map for details.'

Conor glanced at his watch, nodded and instructed them all to put their seat belts. 'Even you, Darragh!' Darragh gave Conor a dirty look and clambered onto Sharav's lap.

'Sorry, Sharav. There are only four seat belts,' Conor said. Sharav smiled weakly. He said it was fine but he looked extremely uncomfortable. Darragh didn't. He looked very comfortable indeed.

'Listen everyone, the gunmen are going to be angry at us knocking them down.'

They heard tyres screeching below.

Darragh started bouncing up and down on Sharav's lap, chanting, 'jump, jump, jump, jump.'

Conor ignored the chanting. 'I'm going to double check it's them before taking evasive action.'

Rachel asked, 'When you say evasive action, what exactly do you mean?'

Just then there was a loud crashing sound as the Mondeo sped through the barrier and skidded to a stop.

'I mean this!' shouted Conor. He threw the gear stick into first and sped towards the edge. Sharav and Rachel screamed, and Paul's eyes were wide with terror. They could hear gun shots behind them. A few metres from the edge of the roof Conor flicked a switch on the top of the gear stick and they heard a loud blast from the rear of the car. They were all pushed back into their seats with the g-force. And then silence. Everyone was quiet as the Mini left the edge of the three-story building, except for Sharav, who was praying loudly. The Mini flew above the three lanes of traffic and headed straight for the canal on the other side.

Conor shouted 'Brace for impact!' The Mini hit the water hard. All the air was knocked out of Darragh as Sharav squashed him against the seat belt. Conor reached for another switch as the Mini slowly sank towards the bottom of the canal. The seals around the door hissed as the Mini became water-tight. After a few seconds the Mini settled on the canal bed. Sharav was the first to speak. 'Are we dead?'

Darragh, having recovered, let out a howl of laughter. 'Are we dead?' he shrieked. 'Are we dead? Yeah, yeah, yeah!'

'Everyone okay?' asked Paul as he turned around to look at the passengers. Rachel and Sharav sat with stunned looks on their faces. Darragh was contented-ly eating his M&Ms on Sharav's lap. Sharav undid his seat belt and pushed Darragh off into the middle seat.

'This is the craziest 48 hours of my life!' exclaimed Paul. 'I mean, are we indestructible or what? I love this!'

'Sure, it's not like this every day,' smiled Conor. 'Anyway relax, we have enough oxygen to survive down here for quite a while.'

Rachel looked at Conor. 'Well actually, suffocating in an enclosed space is not due to running out of oxygen. It's more about being poisoned by carbon dioxide.'

Sharav stared at her. 'She's right! We did this in biology. What was it... normal concentration of carbon dioxide is 0.03ish% and it becomes toxic at 1%. If it gets to 10% we are properly doomed!'

Rachel sighed. 'It's okay Sharav, calm down. Let's work it out. So, this car is about 10 feet by 4 feet wide and 4 feet high. The air has 21% oxygen and each time we breathe in, it uses 5% of that. We breathe out 16%. By my calculations, if there was only one of us in this car, we could last about 9 to 10 hours. Divided by 5, that gives us 2 hours at best. After that, yes, we will die. It wouldn't be very pleasant either. Symptoms would include dizziness, reduced hearing and sight, drowsiness, shortness of breath, headache and then...'

'You are not helping!' interrupted Sharav.

'Look, it's fine,' said Conor. 'Those boys in the Mondeo can't wait around for long. Someone will have called the Garda after hearing the gun shots.

After about ten minutes, I can show you another cool feature of the car.'

For the next ten minutes the car was quiet. It seemed like everyone needed time to think. Paul hated the silence. It was in the quiet that he found his thoughts being drawn back home. He was used to the sadness but now when he thought of home, he also felt a huge knot in his stomach as he worried about where his Dad was. Was he even alive? And why would someone want to kidnap him? He was away from home a lot, but he was just a boring civil servant, wasn't he? Paul remembered the knowing look that Mary had given him when they first met. He was gripped with a sense of urgency. 'We've got to find out who Sabre is,' he thought. 'I've got to save Dad.' Losing another member of the family was too much to even consider and he knew the impact this would have on Mum. Paul remembered the times when he had tried to make his mum feel better. But it was like there was an invisible barrier around her. A wall of sadness that he couldn't get past. It would be so good to see her laugh, to see some of the joy that she used to have. Paul smiled weakly as he remembered how their house had been such a happy place. A place where all their friends wanted to come and hang out.

Paul glanced back at his sister. Although quiet, she was restless. She kept checking her phone and then putting it down, frustrated with the lack of signal. Paul could almost see her rapid, anxious thoughts as she bit her lip and kept glancing out of the misted windows. Perhaps she was worried about Dad too, but Paul sensed there was something else.

Conor broke the silence. 'Okay lads, I think that is long enough. You ready to get outta here?' He touched a black plastic panel near the radio, which slowly moved down to reveal a digital display screen. The headlights came on and they now had about 5 metres' visibility in the filthy water. Two propellers extended out the back of the Mini, the car lifted off the bottom of the canal and to their delight they were propelled forwards under water. Conor smiled, 'I love this car. Bryan, is there a slipway near us?'

'Yes Conor, 100 metres on your right.'

Five minutes later, much to the amazement of the Enniscorthy locals, the Mini exited the water up the slipway. The dirty canal water poured off it. Darragh waved at the spectators as the propellers were sucked back into the car. Conor and Paul opened their windows and they all breathed in the fresh air with huge relief. 'Let's go and catch that boat!' Conor said.

14

FERRY

AFTER BOARDING AT 8.30 pm, Conor handed them each thirty Euros spending money and asked them to meet at the Bernaval Restaurant at 9 pm. Each member of the group had their own cabin. Paul and Sharav headed for their sleeping quarters, which were adjacent to each other. When Paul opened number 15, he gasped. Although not terribly spacious the room was beautifully decorated with gold, cream and dark blue. There were wooden floors, a large double bed, a bathroom and a seating area that held a small table with fruit in a crystal bowl. Paul went straight for the fridge, where to his delight he found several cans of soft drinks and twelve chocolate bars. He grabbed one of the bars and threw himself onto the bed with a smile. Sharav burst into Paul's room with five chocolate bars, one of which was in his mouth. 'Did you find all the chocolate?'

'Got one,' laughed Paul.

Sharav sat down at the small table and looked out at the port. 'What time do we leave?'

'I think it's 9.15.'

'Great, I love ships. Hate planes, love ships.' He leaned back in the soft seat. 'I'm totally knackered. This trip has been wild. Once we have dinner I'm going straight to bed.'

'Good idea,' said Paul. 'I was wondering about letting our parents know that we're okay.'

'Are we okay?' smiled Sharav. 'It's not as if you can tell them everything is fine and please don't worry, we only nearly died four times today!'

'True.'

'Anyway, I'm not sure exactly what part of the world my parents are in. They have had loads of adventures on their trips. But I'm not used to so much excitement.'

SHARAV AND PAUL climbed up a couple of levels and had a look around the ship. Eventually they found the Bernaval Restaurant. Conor and Rachel were already seated at a round table with a white table-cloth, complete with a red flower in a vase and a bottle of wine. Paul looked down at his dirty jeans and thought that he should have changed. Rachel had made an effort. Paul was too hungry to go back to the cabin, so he sat down and said, 'Wow, it's really posh, isn't it?' They heard a loud grunt and looked around to see Darragh push past a waiter and glare at his surroundings. Darragh grabbed an empty chair and threw himself into it.

'Howaya Darragh,' Conor said.

'Urgghhhh,' Darragh replied.

They spent some time looking at the menu. Sharav, having travelled more than the rest of them, was able to explain some of the fancy foreign choices. After a couple of minutes, the waiter approached the table and with the finest of manners took their order, coming to Darragh last.

'And what would sir like to eat tonight?'

'Chips.'

'Of course sir, and what would you like with the pommes frites?'

'Chips!' said Darragh, increasing his volume.

'Sir, we have a large range of delicious meats and vegetables that I'm sure you would enjoy in addition to your... chips.'

Darragh glared up at the waiter, narrowing his eyes and baring his teeth. 'CHIPS, CHIPS, CHIPS!' he shouted. The other diners looked over as he head-butted the table.

The waiter looked at him in shock and quickly said, 'Very good sir,' and scarpered off to the kitchen.

The group spent an enjoyable ninety minutes filled with good food, fun and chat. Conor told them several hilarious stories about his childhood. The waiter had learnt that when Darragh looked at him, that was the sign to bring more chips to the table. After the ninth plate, Darragh smiled at the waiter and Conor interpreted, saying, 'I think he's finished now.' The waiter let out a short sigh and said, 'Excellent, I hope sir enjoyed them.'

At 10.30 pm Sharav looked at everyone and said, 'Well, I'm done. Thank you very much for a lovely meal, but I am going to bed. I plan to sleep until someone wakes me up'.

'Good idea,' said Conor. 'I'll wake you up at about 6.15 am and then we can drive to London.'

As they stood to leave, Paul looked over to see Sharav already asleep, so Conor and Paul took an arm each and dragged him to bed.

AT 2 AM PAUL woke up. Was that a knock? He pulled himself out of bed and walked towards the door rubbing his eyes. He grabbed for the wall as he felt the ship swaying from side to side. Paul noticed something on the floor and knelt down to pick it up. A note. Paul gingerly made his way back to the bed and sat down. 'Hugo, light.' The room was filled with the soft light from Paul's watch. He read the note, 'If you want to see your father again, meet me on the top deck now. Just you.'

Paul's back straightened and he quickly pulled on his shoes and clothes.

Five minutes later he was opening the door onto the deck. Paul took a sharp intake of breath, pulled up his hood and ventured out, leaning against the biting wind. Paul adjusted his weight from one foot to another as the ship rolled back and forth. His eyes adjusted to the darkness and he scanned the deck. He hadn't walked far when he froze as a deep voice said, 'Stay right where you are. Now turn around slowly.'

Paul turned and looked up into the face of a well-built man with dark eyes, black glasses and a weather-beaten rugged face. Paul instinctively edged away from the bulk of the man.

'Stop there please, Paul,' said the man in a strong London accent. 'Smile, you're on camera!' The man pointed to a body cam that was strapped to his chest.

'Where's my dad?' Paul said, his voice cracking with emotion.

'I was going to say somewhere safe,' smiled the man. 'But that wouldn't be true. However, he is watching you right now.'

'Dad?' said Paul looking into the camera. 'I'm going to find you. I'll sort all of this out. I'm fine. I…'

'That's enough,' said the man, grabbing Paul by the neck and lifting him off the ground. 'The whole point of this interaction is to show that you aren't fine.'

Paul grabbed frantically at the man's hands that were clamped around his neck. Now face to face with the man, Paul noticed an image being projected onto the man's glasses. Paul gasped, desperately trying to inhale some air. As he did so, he saw a figure running towards them. Strengthened by this hope he pulled back his right leg and kicked with all his might. The man instantly let go of him and fell to the floor holding his crotch. Paul was on all fours sucking in the cold air and saw the man's glasses had landed nearby.

Conor skidded to a stop near the man, who was breathing heavily on the ground. As Conor got closer, the assailant pulled out a gun and slowly got to his feet. He pointed the gun at Conor. 'This situation has just got a whole lot more serious for you both. I was just playing with Paul here. Putting on a bit of a show for his dad.'

Paul was sitting on the deck, leaning against a bench. Instinctively he grabbed for the glasses near him and put them on. There in front of him he could see his father sitting at a table with his head in his hands. It was like watching television.

'Dad!' said Paul. He felt the prick of tears as he was flooded with relief.

Michael Fox looked up and called, 'Paul... I can't see you. Are you okay?'

'I can see you Dad, I love you!'

'I love you, son.'

Paul saw a bald man rush around the table towards the camera and Michael said with urgency, 'You'll find me at North...' The audio and visual went dead.

'Dad... Dad! Where are you?'

Nothing. Paul threw the glasses aside and stood up.

'GET UP AGAINST the railing,' the man said, finally recovering. He motioned with the gun towards the sea. 'Time to go for a swim,' he snarled.

'I'm sure we could work something out,' said Conor. Paul saw another figure slowly approaching the attacker from behind. As the figure got closer, he could see it was Sharav in his boxer shorts and a t-shirt.

'Listen,' Conor said to the man. 'Tell me what you want. Money? Cars? I work for an organisation that can get anything you want. Anything, just don't hurt him.' He nodded at Paul. 'Let him go.'

'He is the one I'm here for,' smiled the man angrily. 'You are getting in the way.'

Sharav was now within five metres of the group and realised that he had only one option. Taking a deep breath, he ran at the man and jumped on his back. It all happened so quickly. As Sharav was holding on to the man's back, Conor rushed towards him, only to be met by the hard blow of gun metal to his face. He fell backwards and lay sprawled on the deck. Sharav continued to hold on for dear life. Paul joined in and kicked the man hard in the stomach. This resulted in Sharav being catapulted over the man's shoulders. The man staggered backwards, still holding the gun and pointing it at the group. Paul, Sharav and Conor got to their feet and surrounded the man in a triangular formation. The assailant switched his aim quickly from person to person.

'I'm here for him,' he shouted looking at Paul. 'If you want to get in the way, then fine'. He started moving towards Paul and Conor, who both backed away towards the railing. Sharav was now directly behind the man.

Conor looked at Sharav, 'Sharav, protect the package!'

Sharav looked at him in confusion. 'Protect the package?' he repeated.

'Yes.'

Suddenly Sharav understood. His eyes grew wide. 'Surely not now! You said it wouldn't come to this!'

'I was wrong,' Conor said, with a slight tremor in his voice.

'No. This isn't happening.'

Their assailant looked back and forth between

them, clearly unsure of what was going on, but he was still recovering from the kick and couldn't move yet.

'This is happening,' said Conor. 'And it is my job. Him or me. Remember?'

Sharav looked down and took a deep breath. Conor's back was now touching the railing. Sharav looked up and shouted at the man, 'Hey you!' The man looked around, shifting his aim to Sharav. Conor quickly grabbed him from behind, pinning his hands down so the gun pointed towards the deck. Then Conor shouted, 'NOW!'

Sharav rushed forward and shoulder charged them hard into the railings. The momentum knocked Conor and the man over the railings of the ship. As they fell towards the sea two shots rang out. Paul shouted Conor's name as he watched them land in the sea and disappear under the water.

15

HEADQUARTERS

ROB AND NATALIE approached the group who were sitting quietly in one of the ship's lounges. It was 9 am and the *Oscar Wilde* was docked in Plymouth. Rob gently put his hand on Paul's shoulder and asked, 'So how is everyone today?' Paul looked up and smiled at hearing a familiar Scottish accent. No one spoke. 'It's been a tough night, I hear,' continued Rob. Again silence.

It had been a tough night. The alarm had been raised at 2.15 am. The ship turned starboard 180 degrees and its engines were turned off. The staff on board lowered the rescue vessels and a request went out to all ships within 30 nautical miles to support the search and rescue. The RNLI had also been informed. Man overboard. No one was found. Eventually the captain made the decision to continue on their way as planned. The unknown attacker had not been on the ship's passenger list, so there were many questions about exactly what had happened.

Rachel was the first to speak. 'The captain said we had to wait here to speak to the police.'

Rob smiled reassuringly. 'It's okay, I've sorted that. The police are happy to release you into our care. Come on, get your bags, and we'll get you off this ship. Have you had anything to eat?'

Darragh looked at his bag of M&Ms.

'Is that all you've eaten?' Natalie asked. 'We have food in the car.' Since they had heard that Conor was missing, Darragh had become totally withdrawn. He had simply sat on the floor and kept his head down. His face was covered by his black cap and his knees were drawn towards his chest.

Rob looked at him. 'Darragh, are you happy to go back on the next sailing? I think they might let you drive the Mini on the other side.' This piece of information had no impact. Darragh simply nodded his head and stayed where he was. Rob patted him on the shoulder. 'Okay, well, take care. Good to see you and thanks for looking after this lot.'

Paul crouched down beside Darragh. 'Thanks for all your help Darragh, you've been amazing. Hopefully we'll see you again some time.'

Natalie and Rob led the remaining group members off the ship to where three Land Rovers were waiting. 'You can have one each!' Rob joked. No one laughed. 'No, not really. Listen the plan is for you all to go in the middle one.' There were two agents in each car. Rob opened the rear door of the middle car and let them in.

Natalie jumped in the driver's seat and drove off after the leading car. 'It normally takes four hours to get from Plymouth to London,' she said. 'We'll get there in three.'

True to Natalie's word, they were in London three hours later.

'Just a few more minutes and we'll be there,' Rob said. 'Sorry I can't promise to show you the best sites in London. In fact, MI2 is based in Hackney. It's the second most deprived area in England. However, on the plus side there are loads of young people and it is really up and coming. We like it in Hackney because no one expects that a security service would be based here, and everyone just leaves us to get on with it. No questions from the locals. But just to be safe we will be swapping cars before getting to HQ.'

The three Land Rovers swept into a secure car park on the outskirts of Hackney and the group got into a rusty old Volvo and a beat-up Nissan. Soon Rob was pointing out a large, odd looking, orange and cream building. 'There's good old HQ. It used to be a cinema.' On ground level there was a hairdresser, tattoo parlour and snooker club. Rob continued, 'So apparently a hundred years ago there were about seventeen cinemas in Hackney. This one in particular could hold up to 3,000 punters! Amazing really. Anyway, I know it doesn't look great from the outside but inside is a different story.' They parked on a side street and walked up to what looked like the old exit from the cinema. When they got into the hall there was a camera pointing down at them. They heard a buzz and the black door opened. They were welcomed by William, the man who had recruited them. 'Welcome to MI2, it's great to see you all in one piece. Now would you like a bit of time to rest or would you like me to show you around?'

Rachel piped up, 'I could really do with a lie down if that's okay?' Paul and Sharav nodded their agreement.

'Totally understand,' smiled William. 'In that case

let me take you back out of the building to the sleeping quarters.' William walked them to a separate building where Paul and Sharav were shown to a spacious, basic room with two sets of bunk beds. Rachel had a room with two single beds. Within ten minutes of being shown their rooms all three were fast asleep. It was 3 pm.

PAUL WOKE UP with a start. He looked at his watch and saw that it was 9 am. 'Ugh, that can't be right. I just went to sleep for a nap. Hugo have I been asleep for long?'

'Good morning, Paul,' his watch replied. 'Yes, you have been asleep for eighteen hours in total. Oh, and happy new year. Today is the 1st of January.'

'Oh, I missed Hogmanay,' Paul said, rubbing his eyes.

A feeling of dread filled his stomach as he remembered what had happened on the ship. He lay there for 10 minutes before deciding to waken Sharav, who was snoring quietly.

Soon both boys were dressed and Sharav said, 'I'm starving!'

Something suddenly occurred to Paul. 'Hey

Sharav, remember on the boat, just before Conor went overboard?'

'Yeah.'

'Well Conor said something. He said, 'Protect the package… something about me or him.'

'Yeah I do.'

'What did he mean? It was an odd thing to say.'

'Hmm not sure… Shouldn't we get something to eat first?' He looked hopefully at Paul. Paul held his gaze and Sharav slowly sat back on his bed.

'I'm pretty sure that I'm not supposed to tell you,' said Sharav looking down at the floor.

'Listen, Sharav. Conor is missing, presumed dead, and my dad has been kidnapped. I think it's okay to talk about what happened.'

'I suppose you're right. I don't really know all the details, but Conor had a talk with me at the safe house.'

Paul thought back to the safe house, 'Oh yeah, I saw you both outside in the garden having what looked like an intense conversation.'

'Yeah, erm, we thought you were asleep. Conor said he needed to have a chat. He said he couldn't explain everything but that I would need to trust him. He told me that his mission was to "protect the package" and that you and Rachel were the package.'

Sharav looked up at Paul. 'He said that he would have to protect the package no matter what and that it was a matter of national security that he did so. He had been instructed not to tell you because it might compromise the mission and would raise your anxiety. Anyway, he asked me whether I would be willing to help protect you both. I said of course and agreed not to say anything about it. Conor told me that if he needed my help, he would use the phrase "protect the package". When he said those words on the boat, I couldn't actually believe it was happening, but I soon realised that the only option was to charge into the man with the gun. I was hoping that Conor wouldn't get hurt.' At this point Sharav's voice cracked and he was silent.

Paul's mind raced trying to join the dots. 'Are you sure he said that we were the package?' Sharav nodded.

Paul remembered his conversation with his father, and it began to dawn on him. 'These people who have Dad want to get Rachel or me as well. Why is that? Anyway, this is all ridiculous. I need answers. We need to find out who Sabre is so we can save my dad. Come on. Let's go and find someone.'

16

THE TOUR

Soon after, the boys arrived at the canteen. They spotted Rachel sitting beside someone having breakfast.

'Hi,' said Rachel as they approached her.

'Good morning,' said a cheery male voice. Paul and Sharav turned and recognised Rob who was smiling up at them. 'Happy New Year by the way.'

Sharav looked confused. 'Is it the 1st of January?'

Rob laughed. 'Yep, time flies when you are having fun.'

All three of them glowered at Rob who looked sheepish and said, 'Sorry.'

Paul, who was still standing, said, 'Rachel, we need to find some answers.' He turned to Rob. 'Who can I speak to about everything that is going on?'

'Whoa there, cowboy,' smiled Rob. 'You'll get some answers soon enough. Listen, you've been asleep for a long time. I suggest you have some breakfast. William has asked me to show you around the premises. You'll meet the big boss at lunch time. He has asked to speak to you directly.'

'You mean William?' asked Rachel.

Rob smiled, 'No the biggest boss.'

Paul was just about to complain, but his stomach let out a huge rumble. This broke the tension, and everyone laughed. 'Your stomach agrees with me,' laughed Rob. 'Have a seat.'

After breakfast Rob led them back to the main door of MI2. He showed them around with his usual good-natured manner. The ground floor looked like a typical office. There was a reception desk near the front with a receptionist called Ralph, who welcomed them warmly. Behind Ralph, there were sixteen desks arranged in groups of four. Each desk was occupied by a well-dressed young adult working on a sleek white computer.

'So, this is where we can bring visitors,' Rob said. 'There is a meeting room in the corner and these desks are fully manned 24 hours a day, 365 days a year. The majority of the people here are intelligence and data analysts.'

Rob led them up a sweeping staircase to the next level. He turned to the group. 'This building is a bit of an experiment. They have spent a lot of money designing and kitting out the interior on the hypothesis that it will improve people's productivity and ultimately keep the UK safer. I hope you are ready for this.' Rob turned and stooped down to allow the panel to scan his eye.

'This is the green level,' Rob said as he stood aside and opened the door. Immediately they were hit with a wall of heat and humidity. The walls were covered with ivy and moss and there were plants of all shapes and sizes, including bonsai trees that were placed on the natural wooden desks. All the workers were wearing t-shirts and shorts. The floor appeared to be made out of real tree bark. Most surprisingly, there was a shallow river that flowed from one end of the office, meandered around a large tree trunk and disappeared at the far wall. Sharav ducked to avoid a small yellow bird that flew past him. It was busily building a nest above the door.

'They are golden weavers,' said Rob. 'They are great to watch this time of year!'

'This place is beautiful,' Rachel said.

'Yep,' said Rob as he led them to the middle of the floor. The river was narrow enough for them to jump over with a small run-up. 'The employees can decide which level they would like to work on,' continued Rob. 'If they prefer this environment, they can spend most of their time here. On this floor we have a range of staff such as mobile surveillance officers, language specialists, intelligence officers and more specialist roles such as protective security and explosive specialists. Just to name a few. You will be matched to a role when you complete your training. Mr A prefers us to mix as much as possible. He says it's healthier and makes for a better security service.'

'Mr A?' queried Paul.

'Ah yeah, he's the main man. Mr A or "A" for short. He's the Director General of MI5 and MI2 and will be talking to you later. Let's go up a level.'

Soon they found themselves in the cool, quiet environment of the blue level. Sharav was the first to speak, 'Oh wow, this is amazing!' The blue level was spacious, had individual desks, blue lighting and people appeared to be moving slower than on the green level.

'You'll notice how quiet this level is,' Rob whispered. 'It was designed to be a peaceful space, where people can take time to think. The architects cleverly designed it so the sound is dampened. You can get a sense of how relaxing it is.' He pointed out a series of hammocks where people were lying or sitting with laptops and there were also some work pods that looked like huge minimalist pineapples.

In place of the tree trunk on the blue level was a very large grey office with no windows. Rob told them, 'That is A's office space, but we will come back to that later.'

Up on the red floor Paul felt right at home. It was a hive of activity and everyone seemed to be smiling. There were paper lanterns hanging from the ceiling, hundreds of balloons and colourful toys sitting on desks. A small, square robot sped past them. They watched in wonder as the robot delivered a can of Coke to a handsome worker on the far side. In each corner there were novelty offices made out of transport vehicles. Paul's favourite was an office made out of an aeroplane's cockpit. But there was also the front of a London bus, a black cab and an old steam locomotive. Rob brought them over to a games area where a number of game stations were set up.

'Look, this is cool!' beamed Rob. 'Mr A allows video games but they have to be pre-2000 consoles. So in this area you'll find a Commodore 64, Atari Jaguar, Nintendo 64, a PlayStation and a Sega Saturn. All produced well before you were born. The games are surprisingly addictive.' Paul's eyes lit up as he ran his hands over the antique consoles. 'Can't wait to play these boys!' Paul said.

'Okay', said Rob. 'Final level is the yellow level. Let's go up.'

Rob led them to the roof. They shielded their eyes against the sunlight. To their amazement they saw a large group of staff enjoying themselves in a range of activities. Nearest them was an outdoor swimming pool. They looked over the edge and got a surprise when they saw several staff members swimming with three sharks and dozens of tropical fish.

'Don't worry, they aren't actually swimming with sharks. There is a glass bottom to the pool. The sharks and the fish are housed in a tank below the swimming pool. Cool feature though, isn't it?'

Emerging from the centre of the roof, like a graceful hand, was the oak tree.

'How did they do that?' Rachel asked.

'I have no idea, but the tree grows up through the centre of the building and comes out here,' explained Rob. 'Look, there are table tennis tables on each side of the tree. There is also a running track around the edge and of course a pro skateboarding half pipe on the far side. As they reached the half pipe, Rob pointed out a death slide in the corner that could be used to reach the ground floor in a couple of seconds. 'Much quicker than a lift!'

'I've skateboarded before,' smiled Paul. 'Could I have a go?'

'Sure,' said Rob.

'I don't know, Paul, it looks pretty advanced if you ask me,' said Sharav nervously.

'I'll be fine!'

Soon Paul had a helmet and pads on and was managing to skate slowly in the middle of the pipe. He shouted to the onlookers that he was going to try a 360 but would need a bit more speed. He made his way up to the edge.

'This is a terrible idea,' shouted Rachel, but Paul waved away her concerns. He dropped off the far edge of the ramp and the group gasped at how fast he was going. Paul's smile turned to terror. He hit the far edge of the ramp and caught some serious air. He left the ramp far behind. The spectators shouted 'noooooo!', as they saw Paul reaching 30 feet in the air. Paul's heart leapt into his mouth as he could now see right over the edge of the building. Then he was falling. Falling down away from the ramp and Rob shouted, 'death slide!' Sure enough, Paul fell towards the death slide and disappeared into it. Sharav, Rachel and Rob ran to the edge of the slide and looked in. Silence.

17

THE MOONSTONE

ROB SPOKE INTO his watch, 'Get me reception.'

'Calling.'

Ralph, the ground floor receptionist picked up. 'Hello Rob, how can I assist you?'

'Eh, did a young man just come down the death slide and crash into the landing pit?'

'Yes Rob.'

'Tell me he's alive.'

'Yes Rob. He is alive. We are just checking him now. He appears to be unconscious, but he is breathing'.

Thirty minutes later they were all in the canteen again and Paul was leaning over a hot cup of tea. Rachel sat beside him with her arm around him. Rob had managed not to make any inappropriate jokes about Paul nearly dying on the skateboard and instead was being uncharacteristically sensitive.

Sharav used the opportunity to ask Rob more about the training. Rob enthusiastically enlightened them. 'Your training will occur over two to three years. Phase one will take place during the month of January and is when most trainees drop out. You will then return to school until Easter when you will return to HQ for further training. The most intensive training will take place during the summer holidays and will last approximately two months. You will eventually get the chance to shadow agents engaged in real operations. The fun stuff!' Rob beamed. He looked at his watch. 'Okay it's almost 12:15. Time to go and meet A.'

Soon they were on the blue level and were walking towards the large grey cube in the middle of the room. Paul was looking forward to getting some answers. As they approached the cube Rob pushed a section of the wall to reveal a door. He looked around at Rachel and Sharav. 'Listen you two, Mr A will speak to you soon, but he wants to talk to you one at a time. Paul will go first. Is that okay?'

They nodded and Rachel said, 'We'll go and explore.' Rob and Paul went through the door. It closed behind them and Paul found himself in a dimly lit area with a very large black wall just a couple of metres in front of him. He looked up enquiringly at Rob.

'Welcome to the moonstone,' said Rob. 'Not sure why it's called that but some of the agents said it has something to do with A's favourite book. Okay so this is the cool bit… watch this.'

Rob walked towards the wall, lightly touched it and stepped back. Paul gasped as blue luminous writing gradually appeared all over the wall. Paul could see numbers and letters. 'Maths equations?' he asked.

'Yes exactly,' Rob said brightly. 'A is a fan of maths. If you want to get in, you have to write the correct maths equation on the wall.' Rob turned around, picked up a pen that was stuck to the door behind him and handed it to Paul. Rob turned around to leave.

'Where are you going?' asked Paul.

'This is your mission, Paul. Mr A has confidence that you can do it.'

Paul turned back to face the wall as Rob exited and the door closed quietly. Paul scanned the entire wall trying to make sense of all the complicated equations in front of him. The blue writing glowed in the low light. 'It's beautiful,' he whispered. Five minutes passed. Paul started to feel overwhelmed and thought, 'This is impossible, I'm rubbish at maths. I don't even know any equations!' He slumped against the wall and slowly sat down.

'Think Paul, think. What equations do I know?' Then he remembered learning something about Einstein in school. 'Einstein came up with some equation. What was it?' He jumped up and scanned the entire wall to see if it was already there. It wasn't. He walked forward and wrote '$E=mc^2$.' His writing glowed brighter than the other equations and he heard a click. The wall started moving. A crack appeared in the middle. Paul was blinded by the bright light as he stepped inside.

Paul looked around. The office was dominated by the large tree trunk that rose up from the floor and up through a glass roof. Beside the tree was an expensive-looking desk made out of a single piece of wood, on which sat a pen and a neat stack of white paper. There was a wooden statue on the desk and a chair on each side. There was no computer. In fact, Paul saw that this office was in stark contrast with the rest of the building which was full of technology. On one wall there were a couple of paintings that Paul recognised as scenery from the north west of Scotland. It looked like places he had visited on holiday. Paul scanned the room for Mr A. He looked up to see that the office was on two levels. The top level was filled with books on every wall. Then he heard a noise. Paul could see a man's back and watched as he slowly descended the stairs that swept away from where Paul was standing. The man turned around and looked at Paul.

'Hello, Paul.'

Paul stared at him, initially speechless. 'Uncle Stewart?' He finally managed to say. 'Where's A?'

'Have a seat, Paul.' Stewart directed Paul to one of the seats. Stewart looked like Paul. He was tall with striking crystal blue eyes and had dark hair that was going grey at the sides. He had a handsome but weary look about him.

Paul sat down, trying to work out what was happening. Stewart was his father's brother. Paul hadn't seen him since his sister's funeral.

After sitting down opposite him, Stewart smiled. 'So you managed to crack the code outside. Well done!'

Paul said nothing. Stewart continued, 'I'm sorry to surprise you like this. This room is totally secure. No technology. No one can hear what is said here. I'm wondering if you might like some answers?'

Paul nodded.

'Right.' Stewart hesitated. He looked at Paul and then around the room at the paintings, searching for the right words. 'Paul, I'm A. I'm the Director General of MI5 and MI2.' He stopped, waiting to see if Paul wanted to say anything.

Paul continued to stare at him. Stewart went on. 'Paul, your dad is a spook. He's a spy.'

Paul instantly stood up and took a step back, knocking over the chair.

'I'm sorry to hit you with all this, Paul. I thought you and Rachel would want to know. Your dad has been missing for a week now. I'm worried about him and we have had absolutely no contact with him. Has he been in touch with you?'

'Eh, well. I saw him on the ship.'

'He was there?' questioned Stewart.

'No,' replied Paul and he told his uncle all about the fight on the ship's deck and how he had seen his father when he put on the attacker's glasses.

'Hmm,' said Stewart with a worried expression, scanning a single page of text that was in front of him. 'Right, well, we'll need to find out the rest of the details later.'

Paul's mind started racing. His dad was a spy. That was why he was never home. And since his sister Kate had died, his Dad had been around even less. Paul thought about the secret message they got on Christmas Day and what Mary had told him about Sabre. He considered telling his uncle but thought that he'd better keep the information to himself. He said, 'It's hard to take it all in. I suppose it explains why he was never home.'

'Yes, I think he spent more time at work since your sister died. It was probably a welcome distraction.'

Paul's confusion turned to anger. 'A welcome distraction? Do you have any idea how horrible it has been at home? Do you have any idea about how broken Mum is? Me and Rachel have had to look after her. There was no "welcome distraction" for us! We have had to be the adults in all this. She needs to be looked after. By you... by my dad!'

Emotion rushed over Paul like a ball of fire.

'I know Paul, I'm sorry. It's just that work has been—'

'I don't care how work has been or how important you are. I don't care if you and my dad rule the world! We needed help. Mum needs to be looked after!' Paul was now shouting. 'We were abandoned!' He grabbed the wooden statue on the desk and flung it at the tree as hard as he could. The statue split in two. Stewart was now standing watching on in alarm. Paul looked at the wall, shaking with rage.

'I'm sorry, Paul. I don't know what to say. What can I do?'

Paul looked at him with fury in his eyes. 'You can go to hell!' At that, Paul grabbed the sheet of paper on the desk, stormed out of the office, out of the building and started running.

18

RUN

PAUL HAD BEEN running in the rain for an hour, fuelled by rage and confusion. He eventually slowed to a walk and pulled at his clothes as he felt the rain seep through to his skin. As the rain turned to drizzle, Paul pulled out the sheet of paper that he had grabbed from his Uncle's desk. He scanned it carefully.

'Classified. High value targets that may be connected to the disappearance of MI5 officer 5.'

'MI5 officer 5… that must be Dad,' thought Paul.

The document listed several cells, their members and where they met.

Paul spoke to his watch, 'Hugo, where am I?'

'Hello Paul, you are in Peckham.'

'How long would it take me to walk to SE22 8AH?'

'About thirty minutes, Paul.'

Paul broke into a slow jog. He knew it was a long shot and probably dangerous, but he had to do something. The image of his father looking drawn and grey was stuck in his mind. After 20 minutes, Paul slowed to a walk as he approached the dilapidated community building. He whispered into his watch, 'Hugo, are you able to tell me if there is anyone in that building?'

'Yes Paul, scanning... please wait.' A few seconds passed and then Hugo said, 'Paul, there are three people inside the building and two outside at the far end.'

Paul evaluated his options and then ran towards the ill-lit side of the building. He tugged on the drainpipe and started scaling the pipe up to the roof. Paul eased himself across the sloped roof as quietly as possible and slowly crawled towards the edge. He stopped a metre short and lay down, creeping as close to the side as he dared. Plumes of cigarette smoke floated past his head and Paul craned to hear what the people below were saying. Initially all he could hear was the noise of his own heart. He slowed his breathing, telling himself to relax. As his heart rate dropped, he was able to tune in to the conversation.

'How's the missus?'

'Eh, I think she hates me!'

'Ha ha, why?'

''Cause I'm never home, I think. Joe's been making me spend all my time here, preparing for D-day.'

'I know how you feel. I have to head back up to Jock land again soon. I hate that place!'

'Why you going up there?'

'The Northern cell haven't been able to make T2 talk. They've tried everything, even tried to get his kids. So anyway, I'm going up to lend a hand.'

The smoke continued to drift past Paul. He shifted his position and rubbed his nose as he felt the beginnings of a sneeze. 'Oh, not now,' thought Paul as he moved away from the edge. It was definitely happening. Paul held his breath as the sneeze erupted in his mouth. With the sudden jolt Paul lost his grip on the roof and he started to slide to the left of the building. He was picking up pace. Someone shouted. The men had heard him. 'Got to get out of here!' thought Paul as he prepared himself to jump from the edge of the building. Paul reached the edge and jumped out as far as he could, aiming for the white van beneath him. He landed heavily on the roof. The sound echoed loudly in the car park. He slid off the van and looked behind him. Five men now. Chasing him.

'I can't let them catch me!' thought Paul. Paul's feet pounded the path, faster than he had ever run before. After a few minutes he saw a sign for a park and ran towards it. 'Get cover,' he thought.

Paul spotted a band stand and ran towards it. He threw himself down on the other side of the band stand, panting heavily. After a minute, he dared to look over the small barrier. No one was there. He sat down heavily, holding his chest. 'Those men know where my Dad is,' he said quietly between breaths. 'And he's in Scotland… Was that what Dad meant by, "you'll find me in North"?'

Two minutes passed and Paul decided to move. Before he could look again, he heard footsteps. They were getting closer, he had to look. Paul peeked over the barrier and to his horror he saw the five men walking purposely towards him. He turned and sprinted in the opposite direction. Looking behind him, he saw them all running after him. Panic set in. Paul looked frantically around him for an escape. A large cluster of trees. He ran towards them. He jumped over a small bush and smashed his way through the undergrowth. He felt the bramble thorns cut his skin. Zigzagging through the trees, he stumbled and fell but was quickly on his feet again. He could hear the men noisily pursuing him. 'Run, Paul, run,' he told himself. As he approached the edge of the small forest there was more space between the trees, so he increased his speed. Finally, he was out in the open again. But then, bang! One of the men rugby tackled him from the side. Paul lay on the ground gasping for air, unable to move. The five men surrounded him. One of them picked him up and held his arms behind him with a vice-like grip. They escorted him to the other side of the park. As they were walking towards one of the exits, Paul could see a young woman approaching them with a dog.

The man holding him whispered in his ear, 'One word and you're dead! Act natural.' At that he let go of Paul's arms and they casually walked past the woman.

The woman, who was wearing a baseball cap and a tracksuit, looked at Paul. With obvious concern in her eyes, she spoke directly to him. 'Oh, you poor thing. Did you cut yourself?'

'It's fine,' one of the men said reassuringly. 'We'll patch him up.'

'Don't worry,' said the lady, 'I'm a nurse. I'm sure I have some wipes and plasters in my bag.' She approached Paul as she rummaged in her bag. 'Let me have a look at you.' She took Paul's face in her hands and tilted his head up so that his eyes met hers.

Meanwhile the men were looking around them, wondering how to get out of the park without raising suspicion. There were a few more dog walkers around now. They had no choice but to allow the lady to fuss a little before getting Paul out.

The woman sat Paul down on a nearby bench and inspected the scratches on his face. She leaned closer to Paul and sounding surprisingly familiar, she whispered, 'Put these in your ears if you want to live. Trust me.' She slipped a couple of soft ear plugs into his hands. 'Now' she whispered urgently. As Paul was discreetly lifting his hands to his ears, she turned and looked at the men. 'He is in a terrible state. Do you want me to take him back to my house to get patched up?'

'Listen lady, it's nice of you, but we are going to

look after him. We have a van just outside the park. So, if you'll excuse us.' The men walked menacingly towards her. She let them through and, briefly pausing to insert her own ear plugs, spoke into her watch, 'Maximum decibels.'

Immediately the men put their hands to their ears. Three of them fell over and two started running away from the horrendous noise coming from the woman's watch. She grabbed Paul by the arm and marched him out of the park. As they left, she handed the lead back to a homeless man, thanking him for the loan of his dog, and gave him twenty pounds. They jumped into a nearby car and sped off down the street. After five minutes the woman pulled over and looked at Paul.

'It's Natalie, Paul,' she said taking off her cap.

Paul looked at her. 'Oh it's you, I thought I recognised your voice. Thanks for saving me.'

'No problem. Those men are going to experience some serious hearing loss,' she smiled, tapping her watch. 'Actually, all their ear drums will have ruptured. I just exposed them to 150 decibels. I'm glad I caught up with you in time, as I'm pretty sure that wouldn't have ended well.'

Paul was sweating, his breathing was irregular, and he felt dizzy.

'Paul, you look terrible. You are probably going into shock.'

'I'm fine,' Paul said.

Natalie nodded, 'Okay, we need to get you back. Are you okay to go back to HQ?' She started driving again.

'Not really,' said Paul.

'I know Paul, but it isn't safe out here. As you saw it's dangerous out on your own. Especially for you.'

'It never used to be dangerous for me.'

'Yes, well A, I mean your uncle told me about your conversation. So, you know who he is… and who your dad is.' Natalie looked over at Paul. 'That must have been a lot to take in.'

Paul nodded.

'Paul, I'm sorry about all this but it's real and we need to deal with it. As you know, you and Rachel are the package and we need to keep you safe. It would seem that since your father disappeared you are both a target. Some organisation or cell desperately wants to get hold of you. If they wanted you dead, I think you'd be dead already. They want you alive for some reason.'

Paul sat quietly in the car for the rest of the trip back to HQ, trying to process all that had happened. In the end he gave up thinking about it all and stared out of the window at the London lights.

William, Rachel and Sharav greeted Paul back at base. Rachel gave him a long hug, but only after sharply telling him how stupid he was and that he could have got himself killed. William asked Paul if he would like to speak to Mr A.

'No,' said Paul firmly.

'Okay, no problem,' said William. He looked at Sharav and Rachel. 'Get him something to eat and look after him, will you?'

19

THE STAGE

THE DAY AFTER Paul's attempted kidnap he had a chat with William. William was kind and listened well. The conversation helped Paul articulate his confusion and anger about the situation he found himself in.

'I'm not sure I can do this,' said a subdued Paul.

'I know it's hard, Paul, you might need a couple of days to get over the shock of what has happened. You've got a couple of options. I will support you, whatever you decide to do. You can stay here and complete the winter training or go home and spend time with your mum, obviously with the protection of a couple of agents. Listen, you may have worked it out, but your mum knows you haven't joined the Army Cadet Force. She's always known Michael and Stewart are spies. It might help to have a conversation with her before making a final decision.'

William left Paul, who now stared at his phone

for five minutes before finally picking it up. He took a deep breath. Most of the conversations with his mum recently had been stilted and hadn't gone well.

'Hi, Mum.'

'Hello, Paul, how are you?'

'Not bad, I suppose. How are you, Mum?'

'I'm okay, you know. I've been to the library to-day.'

'Oh, that's good. Any news about Dad?'

'No dear, sorry.'

'I spoke to Uncle Stewart,' Paul said quietly.

'Right, yes…. How is Stewart?'

'Fine. I know he's a spy. I know Dad is a spy.' There was a long pause.

'Hmmm. Yes, that's right. You know.'

'Yeah I know, and it didn't really go that well. I got angry.'

'I understand, Paul,' said his mum with a tone that suggested she was now thinking and speaking with more clarity.

Paul felt a lump in his throat as he battled to fight back the tears. 'Mum…. I'm confused. Everything I used to know seems to have exploded in my face. I want to run away from everything, but I can't. Things don't feel safe now. I'm not sure whether to come home or to stay here.'

'My dear son. I love you so much.' She paused. 'I'm sorry that I've been so distant.' Paul couldn't hold back the tears anymore and started crying quietly. Mum continued, 'Of course I want you near me. Knowing you are in the house is a great comfort. But you'll have to trust me on this one. I think you should stay. Paul, I've often thought that growing up is a bit like being on stage. When you are young you get to play safely behind the curtain. It's familiar and all is well. But as you get older the curtain starts to open, very slowly. At first you only get a glimpse of the lights, the colours, the new people. Whilst there is often uncertainty and sadness on the other side of that curtain, there is also so much possibility. There is adventure and hope. With the curtain fully open you can fulfil your destiny.' Her voice trailed off slightly. 'My dear Paul. I'm sorry that the curtain on your childhood has opened a little too soon and a little too wide. I think you should stay because this might well be your destiny. You said that it feels unsafe. It is. But your uncle, and perhaps you, can make it safer. That, my lovely boy, is a noble and worthy calling. Why don't you stay for your winter training and I'll see you in February? If you come home now, all you will do is worry about your father.'

Paul wiped the tears from his eyes. 'Okay, Mum. I'll stay.'

'Good boy.'

'Thanks for talking. Can I phone you again soon?'

'Anytime, my dear.'

Two days later Paul, Sharav and Rachel walked into a large lecture theatre filled with young people. There was a buzz of excitement as the new recruits anticipated the start of the winter training. The only vacant seats were at the front, so the three of them reluctantly made their way forward and sat down. Soon William and four other adults came into the room and walked to the front. Paul recognised William, Rob and Natalie but hadn't seen the other two before. William stepped forward, smiling at the audience.

'Welcome, everyone. Welcome to the MI2 training school. I'm here to tell you a little bit more about what to expect and to introduce you to the team. My name is William and I am the Deputy Director of MI5 and MI2. My remit includes cyber counter-espionage, Northern Ireland counter-terrorism and as you know MI2. To my left is Rob Montgomery. He heads up the intelligence officer development programme. Beside him is Esmee Mirren.'

All eyes turned to look at the stiff backed, sharp nosed, red haired woman whose thin lips were clamped shut in a straight line.

'Esmee leads on intelligence and data analysis. Then we have Dominik Richter who will teach the majority of the technology modules.' Dominik stepped forward, shaking his head. He looked like a wild professor with white hair that stuck out in all directions and staring green eyes. He had oily skin and wore an oversized brown corduroy jacket and grey trousers with what looked like a grass stain on one knee. Dominik cleared his throat.

'No. Two corrections please!' The audience noticed Dominik's strong German accent. 'First correction. My name is Dominik Dunkel Richter. I can see you are all very interested to find out what the names Dunkel and Richter mean?' He looked up, wide-eyed, glaring at the young people. Everyone stared back at him. 'Vell I vill tell you. In German, "Dunkel" means "dark" and "Richter" means "judge". Dark judge if you like. I can see that you are liking that name.' He smiled broadly, scanning the audience. No one smiled back. 'Yes, now second correction. I lead the technology development, but I also take the rigorous physical training and self-defence classes.' Paul whispered to Sharav, 'I can't believe he does the self-defence. He looks like a burst teabag!'

'First years, indicate to me if you think you are physically fit,' Dominik said with a flourish of his right hand.

Initially only a few hands went up, then more followed. Over half of the audience had their hand in the air when Dominik let out an explosive cackle. 'Ha ha ha NOOOOOOOOOO!' Dominik's face went red. 'You think you are fit. You are not. I look at you and see you are fit like a group of unfit slugs.'

'Thank you, Dominik,' William interrupted. He raised his hands in a calming motion. 'What Dominik is trying to say is that the physical programme in MI2 is very demanding.' William looked to his side again. 'So last but not least, we have Natalie Harper. Special agent Harper is one of our field agents in MI5 but also has overall responsibility for our first years in

MI2. Now do any of the other course leaders want to say anything? How about you, Esmee?' Esmee's eyes narrowed and her lips became thinner as she reluctantly stepped forward. 'She is so scary,' whispered Rachel.

There was a short pause and then Esmee said, 'It is lovely to see you all, so it is.' The recruits looked at each other in astonishment. They had expected a sharp, unpleasant voice to come from her thin lips. Instead what they heard was a warm, gentle Northern Irish accent. Esmee continued. 'We are going to have great craic here in MI2 learning how to analyse data and come up with beautiful solutions.' Her tone and warmth embraced the audience like a soft, fresh towel. Some of the audience laughed quietly with surprise.

William smiled, knowingly. 'Listen, first years, if you look behind you, you will see our motto.' He pointed towards the back of the lecture theatre, at the Latin words on the wall, 'Pro libertate. For Freedom. That is the core value of MI2. Freedom. We are here to protect the freedom of the citizens of the United Kingdom, whom we serve. Freedom that many take for granted. Freedom to live and prosper in a country that tolerates differences, celebrates choice and upholds peace. However, my young friends, our enemies are many. They want to undermine our society and tear us apart. They use terror in an attempt to destroy our democracy and we must not accept that. David Crossman once said, "When you give in to bullies, you don't just empower them, you encourage whatever methods they employ to achieve their ends; usually terror and violence." We will not be bullied into submission. We are here to fight back. MI2 is an essential part of that fight. We must be stronger, faster and brighter than those who wish to destroy us. There are 80 young people in this room. Our new recruits. You are here for a reason and you should be congratulated for getting here. You are a talented group, but you must remember that talent will only get you so far. Talent without character is meaningless. The pass rate is low and the dropout rate is high. We are looking for the best and we need young people with fire in their hearts. Fire to make a difference and to protect the people.' He paused and was about to continue when a couple of people in the audience started clapping. The clapping spread until the entire group was clapping loudly in response to

William's rousing speech. William looked embarrassed and signalled for them to quieten down.

'Thank you. One last thing. MI5 is often referred to as "Box 500" or "The Box". In part, this was due to its wartime address, which was PO Box 500. At MI5 we refer to MI2 as the "mini box". The box is an apt name for these organisations because when you work here, it can feel a bit like living in a different world. Those outside this world can't and don't get to understand it. It may therefore feel a bit insular. You can't tell anyone that you work here. This is for their protection and yours. If you are found to have shared your position with the outside world then you will immediately lose your place here at MI2. Your cover story will be that you have joined the Army Cadet Force and have to attend regular training events. Any questions?' Looking around William saw that there were none, so he continued.

'Right, you have four weeks of intensive training until the end of January. Get stuck in. I'm sure you will have fun as well. Now off you go.'

20

SHOPPING

DURING THE NEXT couple of weeks, the recruits were trained in a range of skills that MI2 operatives would need. Paul had taken Mary's advice and was working hard, knowing that the more he learnt about the world of spies the more likely he was to find his father. He was regularly overcome by crushing worry about his father, but he coped by pushing it down and trying to distract himself. Paul often tried to put all the pieces of the puzzle together in his head, 'So, Dad is a spy and he's been captured. The gang who have kidnapped him really want to get some information out of him, but Dad won't talk. So the gang have tried to kidnap Rachel and me in order to make Dad talk. Perhaps as long as we are safe, the gang will keep Dad alive.' But Paul knew that wouldn't last forever. 'Where was he? Dad didn't get to finish his sentence…' Paul tried to remember. 'Did he say,

"You'll find me up North" or was it "at North… something"?' The gang members at the community centre certainly seemed to be talking about Dad and one of them was going up to Scotland. But what about this Sabre? That was the original clue. We need to uncover Sabre.' Paul had been keeping a close eye on as many agents and employees of MI2 and MI5 as possible, but there wasn't anyone acting suspiciously.

Paul buried his thoughts and, driven forward by an inner determination, he kept learning. Paul was naturally gifted but particularly excelled in fitness, close combat and surveillance. He had also shown he could make quick and accurate judgements. Paul enjoyed Rob's sessions the most. Rob taught them how to carry out surveillance on foot, how to lose a tail if you were being followed, how to lie when under interrogation and how to break into houses. Burglary wasn't something Paul expected to be taught, but he found that it was a particular strength of his. He quickly mastered lock-picking and had a flair for bugging houses by installing microphones and cameras.

Rachel was naturally drawn to Esmee. Esmee quickly warmed to Rachel and they could often be found talking in the canteen about their shared passion of analysing intelligence and data. 'Without analysis we are doomed,' Esmee would often say with a gentle tone.

Paul and Rachel just about tolerated Dominik Richter's classes. But Sharav strangely enjoyed them. Sharav acknowledged that Dominik was eccentric and unpredictable, but he was able to put up with his quirks because Sharav loved the technology. Technology made sense to him. It was black and white, ones and zeros, on or off. Sharav was engrossed as they got to learn about cyber security, hacking and cyber espionage. He had a lot to learn but he knew this was an area he wanted to find out more about.

AFTER A COUPLE of weeks William called Paul, Rachel and Sharav into his office.

'You three have done well so far. Really well. The entire training team has been impressed by your skill and commitment. In fact, Rob has recommended that the three of you access what we call our accelerated development programme.'

The 12-year-olds looked at each other.

'That basically means you will access all the regular training but will have more opportunity to participate in additional field work. Nothing dangerous at first but the live field work will certainly sharpen your skills and knowledge. It's an opportunity to learn from the best. Anyway, are you all up for that?'

Did that mean they would have less time to work out who Sabre might be?

'I'm not sure,' said Paul. 'I'm really keen to get back up to Scotland soon and see my mum.'

Rachel shook her head. 'Paul, we need to do this. It's a great opportunity. William, we'll do it.'

Paul looked over at Rachel, surprised at how firm she had been.

'Right, well perhaps you could give it a go first of all. Rob has suggested a great opportunity that's coming up tomorrow to spend time with the Royal and Specialist Protection Team. The RaSP team are a specialist unit of the Metropolitan Police who provide armed protection for royalty, the Prime Minister and other VIPs who are potential targets.'

Sharav tried to stifle a 'Wow,' but it came out loud and clear.

'I'm not sure what they are up to on Friday but

whatever is happening, I'm sure you will enjoy it,' said William.

THE DAY ARRIVED and the three teenagers were dropped off at the RaSP headquarters at 10 am. They were met by a very tall, thin man with a strong London accent.

'I'm Sergeant Adam Palmer and I'll be showing you the ropes today. You can call me Sergeant Palmer.'

Sergeant Palmer towered over the three young people. They looked up at him as he continued to talk unsmilingly. Paul caught a glimpse of his Glock 9mm pistol barely concealed inside his suit jacket.

'We are on active duty today, so I expect perfect behaviour from the three of you. And just for the record I am doing this as a favour for William. Personally, I don't agree with taking small people on duty. Follow me.'

Soon they were in the back of a black BMW driven by a woman called Caterina who was, to their relief, much friendlier than Sergeant Palmer. They were driving in convoy with a Land Rover Discovery and were being escorted towards the centre of

London by three white motorbikes. Caterina smiled round at them.

'Good to have you with us today. I hope you enjoy yourselves. How has it been so far?'

Sharav hesitated, 'Well, Sergeant Palmer met us at headquarters. He seemed…' he hesitated again.

'Like a grumpy old git!' Caterina finished Sharav's sentence. 'Don't worry about him. His bark is worse than his bite. Wait, that's not true. He's fierce and his bite is really bad, but he is the best we have. He has a 100% record in protecting VIPs and I've learnt everything I know from him. He's ill-tempered but really good at his job. Anyway, let me tell you a little about how our unit works. You see the motorbikes up front?'

They all looked out the front window and saw one motorbike directly in front of them and the other two taking turns to speed up to the next exit or junction and stop the traffic to ensure the convoy got through.

'They are the Special Escort Group. You will notice that our vehicles will never stop, even at rush hour. Stopping significantly increases the risk of a serious incident occurring. The lead biker is the only one who knows the route we are going to take. He communicates to the other riders where to go next. They used to use sirens but everyone in London is so accustomed to the noise that they don't take any notice. They have gone old school now and use whistles instead.'

Paul glanced at Rachel. He had expected her to be thoroughly enjoying the trip, given all the cool cars and motorbikes involved. Instead, her face was tense and clammy, and she was staring at the back of the seat in front of her. He gave her a nudge, 'You okay?'

Rachel smiled but her eyes didn't. 'I'm fine.'

AFTER A COUPLE of minutes Paul asked, 'So where are we going?'

'We are going to pick up Cirrus and escort her, would you believe, to a shopping centre.'

'Cirrus?' asked Sharav.

'Oh, sorry yeah. Cirrus is our code name for the Prime Minister.' Caterina looked back and enjoyed the look of surprise on all their faces. 'This is a great opportunity for you to see how we protect the most powerful person in the UK.'

'We have come across the PM before,' said Sharav,

smiling at his friends.

Ten minutes later the convoy swept into Downing Street. They turned the car around and waited for the PM to come out of Number 10. Caterina pointed to the rear. 'If you look out the back window, you'll see the Jaguar XJ Sentinel that Cirrus uses to get around. That is a beast of a car. It's worth £300,000 and has loads of additional features. So, let's think. Obviously, it is bulletproof. The cabin is titanium and Kevlar-lined. There is a 13mm explosive resistant steel plate under the body. Oh, and gun ports so that officers can return fire without opening the windows. Also, it has an independent oxygen supply in case of chemical or biological attack. Officers can release tear gas if they need to disperse crowds. Not to mention the high definition TV and surround sound system. Basically, a beautiful-looking tank.'

Then they saw the PM, a couple of aides and three members of the RaSP team walking briskly out of number 10 into the waiting cars. Paul was finding it difficult to contain his excitement as they travelled in convoy through London. What should have taken forty-five minutes took them fifteen. They had been joined in the car by another RaSP officer. Caterina explained the purpose of their trip.

'The PM planned this about a week ago. She is determined to go out and buy a present for her daughter. She has been advised by our unit that going to a shopping centre during the day is high risk and it will be difficult to ensure her safety. She was having none of it and basically told us to "get it done". So normally approximately six RaSP officers would accompany her, but Sergeant Palmer has put nine officers on duty today along with about twenty uniformed police officers at the shopping centre.

When they arrived all nine RaSP members jumped out of the cars and moved in formation around the PM and her aides. Paul, Rachel and Sharav fell in behind them as they moved towards the entrance. There were uniformed police officers at the entrance to intervene if required. The PM spotted the three young MI2 agents and asked for them to come a bit closer. They were pulled into the inner circle.

The Prime Minister greeted them warmly. 'Paul, it's great to see you again. That incident on the big wheel is all a bit of a blur, but you saved my life that day.' She turned to Sharav and Rachel. 'And to both of you. I'm reliably informed that you managed to capture my assailant! Amazing. Now to something just as challenging. Can you please assist me in choosing a gift for my daughter?'

'I'd be happy to help,' replied Rachel.

Soon the group approached a small pop-up shop in the middle of the concourse that had a range of toys and gadgets. The PM was keen to make a purchase quickly. Particularly as Sergeant Palmer had communicated to her in no uncertain terms that the maximum time they had was ten minutes. Rachel helped her search through the toys. She pulled faces and shook her head as the PM pointed out several unsuitable gifts.

Rachel directed her attention to a circular fish tank. There were a number of colourful fish swimming around in the sealed tank. The prime minister cast her eyes over it, asking the shop keeper, 'Are they real?'

'No,' smiled the owner, 'they are robotic fish that have sensors which make them act like real fish.'

'Ah, low maintenance!' exclaimed the PM, 'That's perfect for Sophie. Real fish wouldn't last a week in her bedroom. Plus 10 Downing Street has this pesky cat that has a long history of killing all sorts of creatures. We can't have real fish. I'll take it.'

The PM lifted up the tank, then said, 'Oh it's heavy. Caterina, would you mind paying for this and getting it into the car?' She handed the tank over and turned to Sergeant Palmer, 'Now Palmer, how long have we got?'

'Three minutes, Prime Minister,' replied Sergeant Palmer.

'Right, just enough time to get a card.'

As Caterina took the fish tank, Sharav noticed a small green and red mark on the underside of the tank. 'Where have I seen that before?' he said quietly to himself.

The group moved off towards a card shop and left Sharav standing by the toy stall with his head down. Paul noticed and walked back to where Sharav was.

'What's up? You coming?'

After a couple of seconds Sharav looked up and quietly said, 'Code Red.'

'What did you say?' asked Paul.

'Code Red! PM is compromised!'

'Are you mad, I don't see anything wrong!'

Sharav started running towards the group, this time shouting into his watch 'Code Red, CODE

RED!' All the other agents looked towards him as he pulled the tank from Caterina's hands. He turned to Sergeant Palmer and calmly stated, 'Code Red, it's a bomb!'

21

ACCUSED

THE RASP OFFICERS sprang into action. Sergeant Palmer and two other officers grabbed the PM and sprinted towards the exit. The rest of the officers cleared the way, knocking several people over. The PM's feet were only occasionally touching the floor.

Sharav was left holding the fish tank with Rachel and Paul standing nearby. Sharav very gently turned the tank over and looked at the symbol of a dragon eating a snake.

'Are you sure about this Sharav?' Paul said, sounding stressed.

'Yes, remember we were shown a list of about thirty terrorist organisations? Some of them had symbols. This was one of them. Can't remember the name.'

Sharav placed the tank upside down on the ground and very slowly opened the battery compartment.

To their horror they saw a digital display counting down. It was at 95 seconds.

Rachel let out a scream and said, 'We have to get everyone out of here!'

Paul looked around frantically and spotted something on the wall. He sprinted over to the fire panel and broke the glass. The fire alarm sounded. The crowds started looking around, confused.

'Everyone out!' shouted Paul, 'Out'.

This caused some of the people near them to start walking towards the exit. Sharav looked down at the display, '73, 72, 71, 70, 69...'

Rachel shouted, 'Bomb! Everyone out!' At first the screams came from those nearest to Rachel. Within ten seconds panic had spread throughout the shopping centre and families were sprinting for the nearest exit.

'We are never going to get everyone out in time! People are going to die!' shouted Sharav above the bedlam. Then Sharav grabbed the fish tank and started sprinting towards a side exit. It was a huge shopping centre, filled with bustling shoppers. Paul ran in front of Sharav, roaring at people to get out of the way. Sharav tried to communicate something to Paul, but his words were slurred. He started slowing down and then stumbled. Paul realised what was happening. Sharav was having another episode of narcolepsy. He was about to fall asleep.

Paul turned around. Running backwards he saw Sharav fall forward, so Paul dived towards the bomb. He fell on his stomach with both arms stretched out. The fish tank landed on one hand and bounced. Paul stretched out again and managed to catch it. Paul stared at the tank waiting for something to happen. Sharav was now fast asleep on the hard floor. Paul glanced at the time. 19 seconds, 18, 17. He stood up, grabbed the tank and sprinted for the exit.

Paul burst into the winter sunshine. He was blinded by the sunlight and strained his eyes to find a safe place for the bomb. All he could make out was cars. Sweat was now pouring off his forehead. Then he saw it. A bright yellow skip. He ran towards it. 8 seconds, 7, 6, 5. From 5 metres away Paul hurled the tank towards the skip. Before he had a chance to turn and run, the bomb exploded. Paul was knocked from his feet and his back slammed against a large silver van. He lay there perfectly still as pieces of wood, rubbish and paper fell around him. A minute later, still dazed, he pulled himself to his feet and walked towards the skip. Although scores of car alarms were sounding, he couldn't hear anything, deafened as he was by the blast. Paper floated down around him like an absurd snowstorm.

THE NEXT DAY, Paul, Rachel and Sharav were in a debrief session with William and Rob. They were in a small room with a large mirror. Rachel's eyes were red with crying and Paul was worried about her. He'd rarely seen her cry. All five of them were seated around a white table. Paul wondered why the session was taking so long. At first, they had been interviewed individually and now as a group they faced many of the same questions. William and Rob took them carefully through every aspect of the morning, including what had happened the day before, conversations they had had on the day and very detailed information about the actual incident.

William eventually stopped and sighed and then said, 'Thank you for your patience, everyone. I realise the questioning can seem a little repetitive, but it was a very serious incident yesterday.' He turned to the boys. 'You almost certainly saved the Prime Minister's life and we are very grateful for that. You may go back to the dorms. Rachel, we would like a few more minutes with you please.'

The boys returned to the residential area and spent time unwinding, waiting for Rachel to return. By 8 pm, Rachel still hadn't come back, so Paul went to find out what was happening. He met Rob walking down a corridor.

'Hi Rob, listen, have you seen Rachel?'

'Yes, I saw her a couple of minutes ago. Please don't worry, Paul. She is feeling a little unwell. We have a doctor coming to check her out. She'll be back soon.'

The next day, Paul and Sharav kept a look out for Rachel and got increasingly worried when she didn't return. Eventually William came to speak to them. He took them into a side room.

'Rachel isn't in a good way. I'll be straight with you. We suspect that she may have had a part to play in the attempted murder of the Prime Minister.'

Paul and Sharav were silent for a few seconds and then Paul shook his head, 'What! Are you kidding? Rachel? She's thirteen, she's… small! Why on earth would she do that? Even if she wanted to, there is no way she would go through with anything. She wouldn't hurt a fly.'

Paul turned and kicked the wall hard.

'Please calm down, Paul,' said William. 'Listen, Rachel was the one helping the PM choose a toy for her daughter. From the intelligence we have gathered, the evidence is clear. Rachel directed her to that fish tank in particular. The one with a bomb in it. It is either one amazing coincidence or she meant to do it. We also have the stall owner in custody.'

'Wait,' said Sharav. 'Do you mean to say that Rachel is in custody? Have you charged her with anything?'

'No, not yet. She has been arrested and we can hold her, without charge, for up to fourteen days under the Terrorism Act. She—'

Paul interrupted, 'William are you out of your mind? Terrorism? This is ridiculous.'

'Boys, I'm just doing my job; I know it's hard to believe. Listen, the reason I came to speak to you is because we need your help. Paul, I wondered if you would mind speaking to your sister? She is refusing to speak to us. Not a word so far and we can't help her or move this investigation forward unless she tells us her side of the story.'

Paul agreed to speak to her. Ten minutes later an agent unlocked a door in the basement and allowed Paul into the room. He was shocked to see Rachel huddled in a corner, with an untouched tray of food and drink sitting on a table. She looked so much older and was white as a sheet. Rachel looked up at Paul with tears in her eyes. He walked over and crouched down beside her, putting his arm around her shoulder.

'Rachel. What's going on? You okay?'

She said nothing.

'Okay. I'm right here. I can wait.' After ten minutes he looked at the tray beside them, picked up the glass of water and offered it to her.

'Drink this, Rach. It will make you feel better.'

Rachel looked at the glass and sipped the water.

'Rachel, why won't you speak to them?'

She looked up at the camera that was pointing down at them. Paul saw the red light blinking and understood. He quickly took a piece of chewing gum from his pocket, chewed it, stood on a chair and stuck it over the camera and microphone. Then he took one of the chairs and jammed it under the door handle.

'That should buy us some time, Rachel. Tell me you didn't have anything to do with this?'

Rachel slowly looked up at Paul and then he knew.

'Oh Rachel, no. I don't understand.' Rachel started to sob.

She was crying so heavily now that she couldn't get any words out. By this time someone outside was trying to get in. They were rattling the handle and banging at the door. Eventually Paul pulled the chair away from the door and opened it furiously, trying to make himself as big as possible. There in front of him was Rob and two other agents. He pushed each of them back and then whispered angrily.

'If you lot keep treating her like an animal, she is never going to talk. Give me more time and stop mucking things up!'

One of the other agents said, 'Okay, Paul. You can have 15 more minutes. Don't try to lock yourself in again though, okay?' The agent put his hand on Rob's shoulder, who reluctantly backed off and let Paul return to the room.

22

POP

PAUL WALKED BACK into the room and sat down beside Rachel again, who had stopped crying.

'Rachel, I only have 15 minutes with you. Don't worry, they can't hear what we are saying. Tell me what's going on.'

Rachel was quiet for a couple of minutes and then said, 'Paul, I can't tell you.'

Paul took a breath, trying to remain patient, 'Rachel, I know you don't want to tell me anything, but you are in serious trouble. Like serious, attempted murder trouble. Something is going on. At least tell me why you can't say anything!'

Rachel looked up at Paul and said, 'They said they would kill Dad.'

'Who said they would kill him?'

And then it all started pouring out of Rachel. Like a bottle that had been uncorked. Rachel told Paul everything.

'I don't know who it was. But before we left Dublin, I got a text message. It said that I was to start training with MI2 and wait for further instructions. It said that if I didn't follow their instructions exactly, they would kill Dad and we would never see him again. I really wanted to tell you Paul. I thought that I could carry out some simple tasks and then they would let Dad go. I had no idea how serious it would get! I mean killing the Prime Minister!'

Paul stared at Rachel, his eyes wide. 'What about the fish tank?'

'I got another text message on the morning of the bombing. And also, an email with a picture of Dad. He looked thin and really unwell. The message gave information about the shopping centre that we would visit and what stall to go to and even what toy to pick. I really didn't want to do it, but I thought maybe it was just a bugging device and how bad can it be if they hear what the PM's daughter talks about? I had no idea it was a bomb!'

'Rachel, we have to tell someone! Sabre must have shared the information about where the PM was going to be. You can't take the blame for this.'

Rachel looked at Paul, her eyes beginning to fill again. 'You can't tell anyone! If the mole finds out they will do terrible things to Dad!'

'Yes, but Rachel we have to stop this somehow. There must be someone we can trust. Who can we trust? What about William and Sharav? Is there anyone else?'

Rachel thought for a while and then said, 'Esmee. She is really lovely. I think she is safe.'

AN HOUR LATER Paul, William, Sharav and Esmee congregated in the moonstone office. The group listened to Paul as he urgently yet calmly retold Rachel's story.

'I wish you had told me about Sabre before now,' said William.

'I didn't know who to trust, William,' said Paul.

'It's okay, I understand.'

Esmee sighed, 'Oh now, this is terrible news, so it is. William, I've got to know Rachel really well over the last couple of months. She doesn't have a bad bone in her body, so she doesn't. Her actions, although misguided, can be fully explained by the fear of losing her father. We have to do something.'

She reached out and placed her hand gently on Paul's shoulder.

'I agree Esmee, this is bad,' said William. 'And news of a potential mole is particularly disquieting. However, we have to follow the facts. Rob is leading the investigation and unless he can find proof to the contrary, Rachel will be in a lot of trouble.' He looked over to Paul and Sharav. 'Boys, Rachel mentioned text messages she received from this unknown person or organisation. We have to find those messages. Did she say where her phone was, Paul?'

'Yes, she said it was in her room,' said Paul.

'Okay,' nodded William. 'Esmee, we need to check any communications that Rachel received through email or message. Please could you see if you can hack into her account and retrieve them remotely?'

Esmee nodded.

William continued, 'Right boys, I want you to go to Rachel's dorm and retrieve her phone so Esmee has a better chance of accessing those messages. Oh, and no one is to see you doing this. If we do have a mole, we need to do this off the grid. You might want to leave your watches somewhere safe so you can't be tracked. Apply the training you've received so far to complete the mission. I'd like you to meet back here about 6 pm. That gives you a few hours.'

THE BOYS HEADED off to their dorm to plan the mission. They discussed the options, distraction or deception, and finally decided that distraction would be the quickest and most effective approach. They casually exited the building via reception, talking loudly about going to the shops. Then when the security guard wasn't looking, they sneaked back around to the side of the building. They waited patiently behind a bin for someone to come out from the side door. After fifteen minutes someone finally did. They didn't have much time. As quickly and quietly as they could they reached the door before it closed and they re-entered the building. Up a short staircase they found what they were looking for. The fire alarm panel. Sharav moved down the corridor searching for a place to hide and came across a cleaning cupboard. He gave Paul the thumbs up and Paul then smashed the panel with his elbow and set off the alarm. He sprinted towards Sharav, who was squeezing into the cupboard. After thirty seconds they could hear the noise of people walking down the corridor as they made their way to the exit. The boys estimated that it would take approximately four to five minutes to clear the building. After five minutes Paul whispered to Sharav, 'Okay I think it's clear. I reckon we have about twenty minutes before the fire brigade let anyone back in.'

They moved quickly towards the girls' dorm and found Rachel's room. Sharav started on one side of the room and Paul on the other. Paul raised his voice so he could be heard over the fire alarm, 'Sharav, the phone isn't here.' Sharav looked over. 'This is her room, isn't it?' Paul picked up a photo of his family and showed it to him.

Sharav then said, 'It's got to be here, keep looking.' Just then the fire alarm stopped and the boys knew they had to be much quieter. They spent another seven minutes searching the room from one end to another, carefully replacing furniture, clothes and knickknacks exactly where they had found them.

Paul looked at Sharav and said quietly, 'I don't understand it. Absolutely no sign of the phone.' Sharav pulled Paul's sleeve, saying, 'We've got to go.'

The boys returned to the cupboard and waited for everyone to come back into the building before making their escape through the side door and re-entering the building via the front door.

At 6 pm the group was reunited. William and Esmee listened with grave expressions as Paul and Sharav explained how they had searched Rachel's room and found nothing. Then Esmee spoke. 'This is terrible. I have spent the last three hours accessing all the possible email servers that Rachel could have used in order to locate the emails she talked about. I couldn't find a thing. Not even a trace. I've used forensic computer tools: I've also hacked into Rachel's Internet Service Provider and accessed the backup of her inbox. Nothing.'

William sighed. 'Listen boys, it was worth a try. I'll do my best to have Rachel transferred up to Edinburgh to a secure location where she can be visited by her mum. We need to leave the rest of the investigation to Rob and his team. They will gather information over the next ten days and then, depending on the outcome, she will be charged or released. But I have to say, it's not looking good.'

23

OPERATION HINDS

THAT EVENING SHARAV and Paul were in their dorm. As the mist of shock gradually faded, Paul started to pace angrily up and down the room.

'This is ridiculous. What is going on! Rachel is being framed for this attempt on the Prime Minister's life. The real criminals were obviously planning to hide all the evidence of their involvement and let Rachel take the blame. It was either going to be attempted murder or actual murder. We've got to do something about this, Sharav!'

'What else can we do, Paul? You heard Esmee. There was no sign of any messages and that phone has definitely disappeared.'

'It makes no sense. Right, we need to follow the evidence. We need to fill in the missing pieces.'

Sharav looked up. 'Okay, all the evidence suggests Rachel is guilty. The missing evidence that would help clear her name is the important stuff. We need to get to that.'

'Exactly!' said Paul. 'We don't have long to clear her name. And actually, if we follow the evidence, I think this could lead us to Sabre and then to my Dad.'

'Remember that stuff about digital fingerprints?' Sharav asked. 'There was one class where we learnt that sometimes it is easier to find digital information than physical information. Maybe we should go after that? Although Esmee says it can't be found.'

Paul frowned. 'Hmmm yeah. Well there are a number of explanations. One, the evidence isn't there. Two, Esmee isn't skilled enough to find it. Three, Esmee did find it and didn't tell us.'

Sharav looked at Paul. 'Well we both know Rachel is telling the truth. So, we can rule out option one. In order to investigate option two or three we would need some professional IT skills, which, no offence, neither of us has.'

Paul agreed. 'Yep we need help. Someone we can trust and who has some serious kick-ass hacking skills.' There was a momentary pause then the boys looked at each other with huge smiles on their faces,

'Terry!' they said in unison. At that Sharav fell asleep.

THE NEXT DAY the boys were in William's office early. Paul told William that he was really homesick and wanted to go and see his mum and visit Rachel who was being transferred up to Edinburgh that day. And would it be possible for Sharav to come as well because he needed some company? William paused and eyed them suspiciously. He was quiet, then finally said, 'Okay boys, you can have the leave, but not for long. I'll give you leave for this weekend. I expect to see you first thing on Monday morning for classes as normal.'

THE NEXT TWO days passed like a month. Paul was desperate to get home and meet up with Terry to see what he could do. He recalled the last time he had seen Rachel. She had seemed really low, but Sharav managed to make her smile when he fell asleep and banged his head on a low shelf. They were really careful about what they said to her in the room, because they knew everything was being monitored. As Paul had left, he had hugged her and whispered in her ear, 'Don't give up hope. I've got a plan. We are going to clear your name, track down Sabre and hopefully find Dad.' Paul remembered the hope in Rachel's eyes and immediately felt guilty. He knew he had said too much. Did he have a good plan?

SHARAV AND PAUL spent Friday night with Paul's mum, who was really happy to see Paul and took every opportunity to hug him. Paul felt the loss of not having his watch with him, but they had decided to leave the watches at MI2 just in case their movements were being tracked. On Saturday at 10 am they arrived at Terry's house. They knocked on the front door and a minute later heard a muffled voice coming from inside saying, 'What's the password, strange visitors?' Paul and Sharav looked at each other, confused.

'Is this the right house?' whispered Sharav.

'Yep, number sixteen,' said Paul.

'What's the password, strange visitors?' came the voice again, but quicker this time.

Sharav and Paul stared at each other unsure what to do.

Paul took a shot at it. 'Open sesame?'

The voice on the other side of the door laughed

quietly and said in a lower voice, 'That is incorrect, stranger. Try again.'

Sharav smiled, 'Okay, how about "Alakazam"?'

'That is incorrect, second stranger. You have two more chances.'

'Is that you, Terry? Please let us in!' Paul called out impatiently.

The voice laughed again, 'Okay, how about I give you a special clue. What if I said I have very woolly hair?'

Paul was frustrated. 'Sheep, camel, llama, woolly mammoth!'

'Wrong, you have lost this challenge, please wait.'

Ten seconds later a small piece of paper was passed under the door. Sharav picked it up and read the word 'ulotrichous'.

'Correct!' said the voice, and the door opened. There before them beamed Terry who was wearing jeans and a dinosaur t-shirt.

'Captain and his first mate, you are very welcome. I hope you enjoyed that little game.'

'Well Terry, how on earth were we supposed to get ulotikos,' Paul replied.

'Ulotrichous,' corrected Terry. Actually, I thought

that was very easy. I enjoy unusual words. Ulotrichous can be defined as "having woolly or curly hair."' Sharav and Paul stared at Terry wide eyed for a few seconds before he turned and ran off. They followed him upstairs to his bedroom. Neither Paul nor Sharav had been in Terry's room before. As they walked into his room their eyes were treated to a feast of dinosaurs. Dinosaur bedspread, wallpaper, stuffed toys, anatomical posters, money box and even some dinosaur confectionery.

'Wow,' said Sharav, 'what a lot of dinosaurs!' Sharav went up closer to the wallpaper and pointed at a dinosaur. 'Oh, nice Stegosaurus.'

Terry let out a huge cackle and shook his head. 'I can see why you made that mistake. That is an Ankylosaurus. They are both about 9 metres long, but the Stegosaurus lived around 150 million years ago during the Jurassic period, whilst the Ankylosaurus lived about 66 million years ago.' He pointed at a Stegosaurus and said, 'You can see the difference. The Ankylosaurus had a massive club tail that could break the bones of other attacking dinosaurs. The Stegosaurus had these plates and spines that ran along its back and tail. That leads me on to something even more enthralling.' He pointed at another dinosaur. 'This beauty was—'

Paul interrupted him. 'Terry that is really interesting, but we need to talk about something else just now.'

Terry looked crestfallen, but smiled weakly and said, 'Yes, well maybe another time.'

Terry listened intently to Paul and Sharav as they retold the cover story that they had worked on the night before. They explained that they were continuing with their training in the Army Cadet Force and as part of their development they needed to undergo field training. They had a fake mission which they needed to complete by Thursday. It involved tracking down evidence to free Rachel from a prison she was being held in. The instructors were playing parts and would not break their cover for the entire mission. They were allowed to seek the help of other people outside the Cadet Force but those contacts would need to keep all the information confidential. As the boys explained the objectives Terry's smile grew bigger. He even let out a chuckle when they explained that they needed IT support and they would like to use him as their data and intelligence analyst.

When they had finished, Terry tried to hide his smile, saying, 'One moment please.'

They watched Terry as he put his hand over his mouth to conceal a grin and then left the bedroom, closing the door behind him. A couple of seconds later Paul and Sharav jumped as they heard Terry shout, 'I WAS MADE FOR THIS!' followed by very loud cackles. After the laughing had died down, the door opened and in walked Terry with a straight face. He said, 'Yes, this is very serious. Okay first things first, what is this mission called?'

Paul and Sharav were quiet for a moment, desperately trying to think of something.

'I don't think it has a name,' said Sharav.

'How about 'Operation Sabre?'' blurted out Paul.

'Why on earth would we call it that?' replied Terry laughing.

'Bear with, bear with,' Terry continued as he walked over to the opposite wall and, to the boy's astonishment, tried to do a handstand. He failed several times and kept smashing his legs against the wardrobe. On his ninth attempt he managed an ungainly handstand and then as his face grew a brighter shade of red said, 'This helps me think.'

After twenty seconds he let out a gasp and collapsed in a heap. He stood up, and as he staggered back to his desk chair said, 'I've got a name.'

He plonked himself into his leather chair and said proudly 'Operation Hinds! That's what we should call it. Alfie Hinds was an extremely intelligent British criminal who managed to escape from three high security prisons. During his final incarceration he had thirteen court appeals dismissed, however he eventually won a court case against the officer who had arrested him and went on to get a pardon.'

'Perfect!' said Paul. 'Operation Hinds it is.'

'Okay,' said Terry as he swivelled his chair around to face three high definition screens, 'how can I help?'

24

STINGRAY

SHARAV AND PAUL watched in awe as Terry processed huge amounts of data across three screens. His frenetic activity was interspersed by abrupt questions that he threw back at them.

'Okay, tell me about Rachel's phone. Smartphone?'

'Yes,' said Paul.

'Which make?'

'Not sure.'

'Phone number?'

Sharav looked around for a piece of paper so he could copy the number down for Terry. 'You got any paper?'

'Paper! Analogue. I don't do paper. Just tell me, I'll remember it.'

Sharav smiled and told him the number.

'Okay, let's see if we can locate the phone the easy

way and just hope that these instructors think you're dimwits and have left her phone turned on.' He turned around and smiled at them. 'Of course, I don't think you are very stupid. It's all relative. Compared to me, some people might think you are stupid.'

Paul nodded. 'Terry, it's fine. Keep going.'

The phone network's server was surprisingly easy to hack and after five minutes Terry swivelled round in his chair to face them again. 'Okay, there's good news and bad news. The bad news is that her phone is switched off and therefore almost impossible to trace. The good news is that your instructors obviously don't think you're stupid.'

Paul slumped onto Terry's bed and bowed his head.

'So, it's impossible to trace the phone?' Sharav said, as he sat on the bed and began to nod off.

'I said almost impossible.' Terry smirked. 'The second piece of good news is that this mission has just got a whole lot more interesting. Impossible for most people. Not for me!'

Paul looked up and smiled. 'Okay, so what's next?'

Terry leaned back in his chair and put his fingertips together. 'Let me think out loud. The only way to locate the phone would be for it to be turned on. The National Security Agency in America, or the NSA as most people call them, have been working on this problem for years. The problem of how to switch a phone on remotely. It's a beautiful problem that I've never had to solve but I'm willing to give it a try. You see, smartphones have two computers inside them. The baseband processor is the part of the phone that deals with the radio waves and the operating system processor runs the operating system. When the phone is off, the operating system processor is also off, but there has been some chatter around whether the baseband processor is ever truly off. It could be that it is always in a ready state. This is a reasonable hypothesis because there are rumours that the FBI and the CIA have been able to locate phones when they've been switched off. This is obviously handy if you need to locate a terrorist or person of interest.'

Paul interrupted, 'Terry, I have no idea what you're talking about. I mean the NSA, FBI, the CIA. They must have their brightest and best working on this problem. I just need to know whether YOU can do it!'

'Hold your ponies, Captain. You must allow the flow of thoughts to continue. What we need is to trick the phone into connecting to a malicious tower rather than the carrier's tower. Then we would need to get the baseband processor to interact with the operating system processor.'

Terry swung around to face his computer again. Sharav was fast asleep by this point. Every time Paul tried to ask Terry a question, he would hold his hand up and continue with his work.

Four hours later Paul and Sharav were still in Terry's room and Sharav had been awake for half an hour. They received a text message. 'This could take a while. Please go home. Eat, sleep, drink (not particularly in that order) and come back tomorrow.' It was from Terry. The boys looked at the back of Terry's head, smiled at each other and walked out.

The next morning after a pleasant breakfast with Mrs Fox, Paul messaged Terry to ask how he was getting on. He only received one word in reply: 'COME!'

An hour later they were all standing in Terry's room. Terry was wearing the same clothes as the day before.

Sharav looked concerned, 'Terry, have you slept?'

'Well at 3 am my head did hit the desk. A micro sleep, you could call it. So yes.'

'Are you okay?' asked Sharav.

'Okay as the day is long!'

'Give us an update, Terry. What have you learnt?' asked Paul.

Terry's eyes brightened as he talked through all the steps he had taken to investigate the 'beautiful problem,' as he put it. How he had read hundreds of conspiracy theories online, read through dozens of hacker forums and had a 'quick look' inside some of America's more important agencies.

Sharav raised his eyebrows at this and said, 'Terry, please tell us you haven't done anything illegal or got yourself into trouble?'

Terry smiled broadly, 'I can assure you I will not get into any trouble!'

Sharav was about to say something else but Terry continued on his monologue detailing all the avenues he had explored. 'Amongst all the dross that's on conspiracy theory sites, you occasionally get a nugget or an angle that you would never have considered. However, there are some crazy people out there! Can you believe that some people think that dinosaurs helped build the pyramids or that Michael Jackson was killed by the Iranian government? Or my favourite, that the moon doesn't actually exist!'

The boys laughed heartily together. In contrast to the intensity of the last couple of weeks this was welcome relief.

Paul looked at Terry. 'Terry, what I need to know is whether you can find Rachel's phone.'

'Well my young friend the jobbie, I think it is possible. The FBI use a programme called Stingray to mimic a phone mast, turn the phone on and then locate it. Give me another ten minutes and we can give it a go.'

Paul and Sharav spent a tense ten minutes sitting on Terry's bed. Paul eventually stood up and paced up and down, remembering the promise he had made to Rachel.

Terry suddenly leaned back in his chair. 'Okay, well, luckily the code in the baseband processor has loads of bugs, which has made it easier to hack. Are you ready to execute?'

'Yes!' said Paul and Sharav in unison.

Terry's forefinger hovered over the enter button and then he pressed it. They all stared intently at the screen as a map of the world span around. Twenty seconds later the screen started to zoom in. 'Oh,' said Terry. 'I've managed to turn it on!' The map zoomed in further. First to Europe, then to the UK, then to the boys' relief, Scotland. Slowly the programme homed in on the east of Scotland and finally stopped on the east coast over North Berwick.

'North Berwick!' shouted Paul. 'That must only be thirty miles from here!'

'Twenty-four miles, actually,' corrected Terry. 'I'd estimate forty-five minutes by car or fifty-seven minutes by train.'

Paul froze. The blood drained from his face as he stared at the floor.

'You okay, Captain?' asked Terry. 'Interesting carpet, isn't it?'

Paul put his hand to his forehead. 'Of course, North Berwick. Dad said, "you'll find me in North…", he didn't get to finish the sentence. He was going to say, "North Berwick".'

'Your dad's in North Berwick!' exclaimed Sharav,

studying the map. 'Can you get a more exact location, Terry?'

Terry shook his head, 'No sorry, I've only been able to triangulate the location using three masts, which gives a radius of approximately eight miles. We would have to travel to North Berwick and then hopefully get a more accurate location using my laptop and some cool tech I picked up six months ago. And yes, you may say it now.'

Paul looked at him. 'Say what?'

'I am a genius, of course!'

The boys laughed. Sharav slapped him on the back, 'Terry, there is no doubt that you are a genius. Thank you so much. Right, how are we going to get there?'

'Hmmm, I wonder if my sister is about,' Terry said.

At the mention of Terry's sister, Paul's eyes lit up. All the boys in their school fancied Jessie. She was the total opposite of Terry. She was popular, dark haired, not very clever, but very beautiful. Terry stood up from his chair and walked off purposely.

There was a pause and then an almighty scream, 'GET OUT OF MY ROOM! YOU SMALL-EYED,

GINGER SKUNK!' There was a moment of silence followed by, 'No of course I won't drive you and your revolting friends to North Berwick! Are you mental?'

Sixty seconds later Terry re-entered his room. 'Well, that went well.'

'Do you think?' said Sharav, looking alarmed.

'She's going to take us.'

Paul laughed, 'We heard her screaming and calling you a small-eyed skunk.'

Terry smiled, 'Yeah but I've got something she wants.'

'What?' asked Paul.

'Money! I've said I'll pay her to take us. But she takes about two hours to get ready so let's go down and have some lunch. We have an exciting day ahead of us. I can feel it in my toenails!'

25

NANO

JESSIE WAS INTRODUCED to Sharav and Paul in the kitchen. Paul stood up from the kitchen table and tried to say something, 'I… it…. we saw… I like… I mean… I like your shoes.' Sharav looked quizzically at Paul and smiled before saying, 'Thanks for agreeing to take us to North Berwick.' Jessie looked them up and down like she was surveying joints of rotten meat and then walked off. Terry followed her with a spring in his step and said over his shoulder, 'She doesn't really talk to anyone before 1 pm.'

Jessie reversed her very old Toyota out of the driveway without looking behind her. This gave Paul and Sharav their first clue that Jessie may not be the best of drivers. As they joined the Edinburgh by-pass Terry started talking about how the by-pass reminded him of a particular dinosaur called Dreadnoughtus that was twenty-six metres from head to tail. Everyone jumped as Jessie turned to Terry and screamed, 'NOOOOOOOOOO!'

Terry stared at her.

'Okay, here are the rules,' she continued. 'I will drive you to North Berwick, but I will not tolerate any mention of dinosaurs. Not a squeak! You hear me?'

'Yes, Jessie,' said Terry, looking terrified.

Jessie continued, 'Anyway, I am sure we can talk about something far more interesting. My boyfriend, for instance.'

Terry sighed.

'Joe is so gorgeous… anyone mind if I tell you a bit about him?' Jessie simpered.

'That's fine,' piped up Sharav.

'Okay, great. Well, Joe is gorgeous. Have I said that already?'

As they approached a very large roundabout, Jessie said, 'Oh this roundabout is a bit tricky.' She turned right and started driving the wrong way around the roundabout. The three boys pushed themselves back into their seats and looked in terror out of the front window.

Terry started to scream, 'Wrong way, wrong way.

Abort, abort, abort.'

Jessie ignored him and continued to talk. 'Anyway, Joe is eighteen. He's tall, handsome, strong, yet gentle. And soooo lush.'

'Death is coming, all is lost!' Terry shouted. He started hyperventilating. Sharav fell asleep.

It was only when Jessie saw two cars driving right at them and sounding their horns loudly that she took any notice, 'Oh this is strange. What are they doing driving that way? Stupid drivers!' She weaved one way and then the other, somehow managed to avoid them and took a sharp right leading onto the motorway.

'Wrong way!' shouted Terry again. 'I am too young to die. Goodbye world!' They were headed onto the motorway on the wrong side. Jessie was once again having to weave between the oncoming cars.

Jessie stuck to the left-hand lane, the way her instructor had taught her. However, they were on the wrong side of the motorway in the fast lane. Jessie was beginning to show signs of stress.

Terry was moving his head from left to right really quickly. 'I leave my three computers to my friend

Robert. My dinosaur wallpaper to Phil. I leave £400 to the Palaeontological Association to continue researching my beloved dinosaurs.'

Jessie snapped, 'No dinosaurs!' and she punched Terry between the legs. Terry's head flew forward, bashing off the dashboard.

Paul knew he had to do something. He undid his seat belt, climbed into the front and sat on Terry. Without saying a word, he grabbed the steering wheel with his right hand and the handbrake with his left. Waiting for a gap in the traffic he swung the steering wheel right while pulling the handbrake up hard. The car did a perfect 180-degree turn. He pulled the steering wheel left and shouted 'brake!' Jessie stepped hard on the brake and the car came to a standstill on the hard shoulder.

Paul climbed into the back seat again, smiling at the sleeping Sharav. Jessie rested her head on the steering wheel as Terry started mumbling something like, 'The time has come for all good men to….' His voice trailed off.

Fifteen minutes later they were driving to North Berwick on the correct side of the road. Paul had convinced the traumatised carload of passengers to continue on their journey. Sharav was awake and Terry was now tense and strangely subdued. He recovered as they arrived in North Berwick and opened up his laptop.

'Where do you want to be dropped off?' asked Jessie.

'Not sure yet,' was the reply from Terry. 'Just drive for a while and I'll give you directions.'

Five minutes later they found themselves on a one-way street headed up the Westgate.

'Wait! I've got something!' exclaimed Terry. 'Turn right up here.' Paul leaned forward to look over Terry's shoulder.

The car turned onto Westend Place and then onto Beach Road. To their left was a green space and then the North Sea. Terry smiled and turned round to speak to Sharav and Paul.

'I've got it!' He pointed at a house on their right. 'Keep driving, Jessie. Please drop us off 200 metres up here.'

Jessie dropped the boys off, telling them how lucky they were that she had a friend who lived in North Berwick and that she would pick them up in a couple of hours. Terry pulled on a huge rucksack and the three of them walked towards the house. They decided to walk through the park, so as not to get too close to the house until they had a plan. As they passed the house, they could see that it was an old stone-built house with an extension on the side. It also had a glass balcony on the third floor. They sat down on a bench facing the sea and Terry pulled out his laptop again. They looked up the address on Google Maps to get an aerial view to help them decide how best to get into the building. The house was surrounded by high walls and looked highly secure.

Sharav asked, 'So we are sure that Rachel's phone is in that house?'

'Yep,' said Terry.

Paul felt his stomach churn with a mixture of excitement and worry. Could his dad be here?

'Okay, well, we have to get in there asap,' said Paul.

'Hmm, easier said than done, Captain,' said a serious Terry. 'We don't know how many people are in there or what the security is like.'

'Okay, let's set up some sort of diversion,' said Paul.

'Hold on. I've got another plan,' said Terry as he pulled a small cardboard box out of his bag.

'Oh, a dragonfly,' said Sharav once the box was opened.

'Yes! Sort of,' said Terry proudly. 'this is the latest micro MAV. I acquired it recently after doing a bit of work for someone.'

'MAV?' asked Sharav.

'Micro Air Vehicle. I can control it from my phone. It has a camera, a microphone and some other surprises. We can use this to gain access to the house, check out what's going on in there and hopefully locate the phone.'

Terry turned the MAV over and pressed a button. The dragonfly started flapping.

'That's amazing!' exclaimed Sharav.

'Okay let's try this little fella out,' said Terry. The dragonfly took off from their position and Terry piloted it towards the house. They could see everything from the dragonfly's perspective. Terry made it hover over the back garden where they could see a huge pit bull dog chewing a bone. Terry found a ventilation shaft and flew the MAV into the house, through the kitchen and into the living room, which were both empty. The MAV travelled upstairs into a bedroom and then into another living space with a large television, two computers and a grand piano in the corner. On the piano was a large white, long-haired cat. The cat raised its head as the dragonfly came closer.

'Ugh, I hate cats!' said Terry. Suddenly, without warning, the cat sprang from the piano and took a swipe at the flying object. The boys gasped as they saw the drone tumbling towards the floor. Terry was just about to see if it would fly again when the camera appeared to cut out.

'The cat is eating the dragonfly!' said Paul.

'What? My precious robot!' Terry dropped his phone and started running towards the house.

'Wait, Terry!' Paul sprinted after him and had to rugby tackle him to the ground. 'Terry, we can't go in there.'

'But it's worth thousands of pounds!'

'Okay, let's have a think about it, we need to come up with a plan,' said Paul, as he led Terry back to the bench.

Terry activated the small light on the dragonfly and to their astonishment it turned on. All they could see was what looked like shiny ripples.

'Are we inside the cat's stomach?' asked Sharav.

'Looks like it,' said Terry. 'Right, I need to get it out of there! I'm going to make it fly.'

'In the cat's stomach?' exclaimed Sharav.

'Yes,' said Terry. 'We need to try something.' Terry got the wings flapping. This was followed by some loud rumbling noises. Then the dragonfly was tumbling and suddenly the camera was flooded with light.

Soon afterwards, they heard a couple of men's voices entering the room. 'Ugh, the stupid cat's been sick again!' said a man with an English accent. 'It's your turn to clean it up!'

The other man sighed and said, 'Okay, then.'

Paul said to Terry. 'We need to get that robot flying before they clean up the mess and find it.'

Terry frantically adjusted the settings on his phone and eventually, to their relief, they could see the MAV gain some height. Terry piloted it onto a bookshelf in the corner of the room with the camera pointing towards the door. They could see a large teenager with bad skin sitting on a chair, engrossed in his phone. After a couple of minutes, the other man entered the room. He was tall and had bright ginger hair. As he entered the room he said with a strong English accent, 'Right where's the sick?'

Both Paul and Sharav leaned closer to Terry's phone and said in unison, 'Is that Conor?'

26

INSIDE

'CONOR'S DEAD!' SAID Sharav. 'It can't be him!'

'Terry, can you zoom in on that ginger-haired man?' said Paul.

Terry obliged.

'It's him. It's definitely him,' said Sharav. 'I'm so glad he's alive. I'm so glad. I thought I'd killed him.'

Terry looked at Sharav strangely.

'Sorry,' Sharav said to Terry, putting a hand on his shoulder, 'We'll explain later.'

Paul pulled Sharav away from Terry and spoke quietly, 'How is he alive? I don't believe it, and why is he in North Berwick?'

'With an English accent!' replied Sharav.

Paul stood stock still. 'He must be a double agent working for the bad guys.'

Terry approached the two friends, interrupting them. 'Gents, I hate to break up the confab, but we have a phone to locate. Are you ready to continue?'

The boys agreed and Terry flew the dragonfly out of the room and searched the whole house. Paul held his breath, expecting to see his father at any moment. His hopes were finally dashed as they dragonfly completed the search in the basement. 'Where is he?' Paul thought and felt his heart physically sink in his chest.

TERRY DIRECTED THE dragonfly back up to the top floor. The top floor had a couple of rooms. One looked like an office and the other was being used as a meeting room. In this room, which led onto a glass balcony, they found two men and a woman looking at papers that were strewn across a table. Terry landed the dragonfly on the windowsill so they could hear the conversation.

The heavily built, bald man spoke first, 'After our last botch-up, security will be tighter than ever. They will deploy a ring of steel around the Prime Minister, so we'll need to use our man on the inside to get it done. We have to be clever about this and complete the mission without implicating Sabre. He's our most important asset.'

Paul whispered, 'He said Sabre! Terry, can you record this?'

'Hold on!' said Terry. He handed his phone to Paul, picked up his laptop and put in a set of headphones. A minute late he smiled, 'Right, the MAV doesn't have a recording device but I turned on the recording app on Rachel's phone. Her phone is in that room. And it's now recording!'

The thin, blond woman chipped in, 'I'll be communicating with Sabre in a couple of hours, so we need to work out if we have anything new to tell him.'

The bald man said, 'I think we continue with plan B as we discussed. He may have to get past a few more security officers this time. Once the target has been neutralised, Sabre is to meet us at the pickup zone, and we will help him disappear. Disappear to any country he wants, a much richer man. But it would be good to find out more about how the internal investigation is going and whether they have managed to pin the attempted murder on that wretched girl. She needs to be found guilty.'

Blondie smiled. 'Okay, I'll ask him about it. Sabre is part of the investigation and I'm sure we will get the outcome we want.'

'And if not, she'll need to be neutralised as well. Got it?'

The other two nodded in agreement.

'What about T2?' asked the third person in the room, an older teenager with spiky hair.

The bald man shook his head wearily. 'He hasn't talked. I don't think he's going to. The only way we were going to get him to talk was to capture one of his snotty kids. But that didn't work, did it?' The bald man stared at the teenager with fury. 'Keep him alive as insurance until the mission is complete, then kill him.'

The teenager replied, 'We moved T2 yesterday and designed an ingenious way to neutralise him without us even being in the room!'

Paul stood up, 'They're talking about Dad and Rachel! That cell is responsible for capturing my Dad and framing Rachel… and Conor is part of it. I can't believe it.'

Sharav nodded, 'Yep and they are planning to use this Sabre person to try and kill the Prime Minister again.'

'Okay,' said Paul. 'we need to get in there. There

must be information in the house about where Dad is. The easiest way to prove Rachel's innocence and that they are conspiring to kill the PM is to get that phone. It has all the evidence we need.'

Just then, Terry drew their attention to the fact that the spiky teenager had been told to make some coffee and had left the room. 'I have an idea!' said Terry. The MAV followed Spike down to the ground floor and into the kitchen. 'It might not work but I'll give it a go.'

TEN MINUTES LATER, Terry, Paul and Sharav were at the back gate looking through a gap in the fence at the enormous guard dog. Paul turned to Terry. 'Listen, Terry, it's probably time to tell you that this is actually a really serious situation. It isn't a game. I'm sorry for telling you that it was. This is all real and if we get caught goodness knows what they will do to us.'

Terry laughed quietly, 'Captain, I know. I have been researching the security services for as long as I can remember, and I can tell the difference between a game and real life. I knew this was real when you first described the situation to me. Why do you think I was so excited?'

Paul and Sharav stared at Terry for a moment and then Paul said, 'Wow, you are amazing. Okay Terry, you have to stay here.' He handed Terry a radio device and gave Sharav an earpiece, before inserting his own. 'We need a code word in case back up is required. If we say the code word, then please call 999 and get help. What word should we use?'

Terry stroked his chin, looked at them with a glint in his eye and said, 'How about, "boobie misadventure".'

'What? I'm not saying that!' exclaimed Paul.

Terry folded his arms. 'No boobie misadventure, no backup.'

Paul could see that he wasn't going to win this one. 'Fine,' he said, as he pulled out his lock picks and started working on the lock of the back gate. It was a simple lock that opened quickly. Slowly they opened the gate and Paul poked a large stick through the gap, waving it at the dog. With bated breath they watched the dog look up and slowly walk towards the gate. As soon as the dog got to the gate, Paul opened the gate wide and flung the stick as far as he could into the green space. The dog bounded past the boys after the stick, and both Sharav and Paul snuck into the garden and closed the gate behind them.

'Hey, are you going to leave me with that dog!' said Terry with his back to the gate. But Sharav and Paul were already at the back door.

Paul touched his ear, 'Terry, how long before we are safe to go in?'

Terry, who was trying to wrestle the stick from the dog sounded out of breath, 'It only takes about ten minutes to take effect, so in sixty seconds you should be fine. Remember we only managed to get to four of the team. That leaves one of them fully functional.

Before reaching for the door handle, Paul turned to Sharav and whispered, 'Remember, try to be as quiet as possible! We want to get in and out without being detected.' Sharav nodded.

To Paul's surprise the back door was unlocked. They opened the door and entered the kitchen. Slowly they tiptoed into the hall. The house was still, apart from the slight murmur of conversation a couple of floors up. They walked silently along the carpeted hall floor and turned to go up the first flight of stairs. They heard Terry's voice through the radio earpiece. 'Okay me hearties, I'll be your lookout. Your buccaneer in the crow's nest of your pirate ship. The three baddies are continuing their meeting on the top floor. They are happily drinking their coffee. They all seem strangely fine so far. Give me a minute and I'll check the whereabouts of the other two.'

Paul and Sharav froze halfway up the stairs waiting for further guidance from their eccentric friend. Moments later Terry continued, 'Okay so your double crosser, Conor, and the fat, spotty one are having a chat in the cat-sick room. The door is open but they won't be able to see you as you pass. This is fun!'

Paul wasn't finding it so much fun. He was terrified of being captured because of what it would mean for his sister and his dad.

They continued up the stairs and sneaked past the living room door, continuing their way to the next flight of stairs. This flight of stairs had a number of pictures on the wall. Paul reached a mini landing with a small table and vase in the corner. He passed it and turned around to point out the obstacle to Sharav. But to his horror Sharav's leg touched the table and it wobbled slightly. The vase moved one

way and then the other. Paul tried to barge past
Sharav to catch it, but it was too late. The large,
expensive-looking vase bounced on the landing and
started falling down the short flight of stairs to the
bottom. It didn't make a lot of noise until it got to
the bottom and smashed loudly against a bookshelf.
Panic. Suddenly they were faced with two men from
the upstairs room. The bald man shouted, 'Oi, who
are you?' Paul turned around and pushed Sharav in
the opposite direction. 'Run,' he shouted.

27

THUMB SCREWS

Paul and Sharav were bounding down the stairs two at a time. They were being pursued by the bald man and Spike the teenager. Just as they reached the living room on the first floor, the large spotty teenager jumped in front of them and they ran into his open arms. 'Hello boys,' he said as he grabbed them tightly. 'Where are you off to in such a hurry?' Baldy and Spike caught up with them and they were bundled into the cat-sick room. And there was Conor.

Conor looked at them wide eyed for a moment before saying, 'Who are they?'

Baldy replied, 'I'm not sure, but we are going to find out.' Paul and Sharav were shoved onto a sofa. All five members of the gang were staring down at them. There was no escape. Baldy came over and grabbed them by the scruff, pulling them to their feet. 'I don't like people coming into my house without permission! Who sent you?'

Paul and Sharav looked up at him and Paul frantically tried to remember his interrogation training. He was breathing quickly and tried to calm his thoughts. He stayed silent.

Baldy turned to Spike and said, 'Tie them up.'

Spike approached them, smiling. 'It's okay boys, we have ways to make you talk. Ways that I really enjoy.' He pulled two cable ties from his pocket and within seconds both Paul and Sharav had their hands tied painfully behind their backs.

Baldy stood close to them and smiled. 'Boys we can do this the easy way or the hard way. Spike here has a way with people. He gets them talking no bother at all.' Baldy was now inches away from their face. 'WHY ARE YOU HERE?' he shouted. Silence. Then with a rush of temper he punched them both in the stomach. They were knocked back on the sofa, gasping for air.

Terry, who had piloted the micro drone into the living room was watching everything and started to panic. 'Captain, you okay? You want to use the special code word? Just let me know and I'll get help.

Say it!'

The bald man noticed something in Sharav's ear. He reached down and pulled out the earpiece and then quickly turned Paul over and grabbed his one as well. 'Oh, this is more serious than I thought,' he said, as he dropped the earpieces on the floor. Sharav tried to suck enough air in and shouted 'boobie misad…' Baldy crushed both earpieces with his heavy boot. He looked at Sharav and said, 'What was that, boy?' Sharav closed his mouth and looked down.

Baldy turned to Spike and said, 'Make them talk.' Spike smiled a sickly smile and left the room. Meanwhile Paul stared at Conor, his face getting red with rage. Now face to face with Conor, Paul wanted revenge. He had recovered sufficiently from the punch to say through gritted teeth, 'You betrayed us! I'm going to make sure you pay for this. We trusted you!' The gang looked from Paul to Conor.

'Do you know him, Phil?' The blond woman asked Conor.

'I don't know what he's on about,' Conor replied in a strong London accent. 'Never seen them before. Now let's get them talking.' He walked up to Sharav and Paul and slapped them hard across the face.

Baldy pulled them back to their feet just as Spike returned carrying two small metal devices. Spike turned to Blondie, 'I'm going to need their hands for this, can you cut them loose?' Blondie grabbed Paul and then Sharav and cut the cable ties with a large knife.

Spike explained what he was going to do. 'The old forms of torture are the best.' He placed Sharav and Paul's thumbs in two vice-like contraptions and started turning the screws. 'These are called thumb screws. They were used in medieval Europe around the 1600s to extract confessions from people who they thought were witches. It's a simple device that basically crushes your thumbs. Extremely painful. I'm hoping you don't talk.'

Paul and Sharav looked at each other. Their hands were held out in front of them and each thumb was secured in the thumbscrews. It was becoming very painful when something unexpected happened. Spike, who was turning the screws, began to laugh. At first the gang started laughing along with him, but after twenty seconds they stopped and looked enquiringly at Spike. Spike had now stopped turning the screws and was bent over, slapping his knees in hysterics.

Baldy said, 'What's so funny? Don't you think you're enjoying this a bit too much?' After a minute Spike fell on the floor gasping for breath as his laughter continued.

'I don't know what's wrong with him,' said the blond woman. As she approached the boys to tighten the thumb screws she sneezed. She looked surprised. Then she sneezed again, then again and couldn't stop. She was sneezing every couple of seconds and had to back away and sit down.

Baldy looked at both his gang members in disbelief. 'What's going on?' Then Spotty said, 'Boss, I don't feel too well. I'm just going to visit the loo.' Sixty seconds later they could hear a huge diarrhoea explosion coming from the bathroom across the hall, along with heavy groans. Then another diarrhoea explosion, followed by four or five more. Baldy shook his head. 'You better not have anything to do with this!' he said as he approached Paul and Sharav menacingly. He asked Conor to hold Sharav. As he was about to turn the thumb screws, Baldy collapsed to the floor and before long was snoring peacefully on the carpet. Ten seconds later he woke up, jumped to his feet and rubbed his eyes. 'Listen you two, how is this happening? Did you drug us?'

Paul smiled, 'Yep, with my friend's trusty drone.'

Baldy pulled his large arm back and clenched his fist. Paul winced as he saw the fist flying towards him. Mid punch, Baldy fell backwards hitting his head on the floor, again fast asleep. Paul used the distraction to throw his head back hard, smashing it against Conor's nose. Paul and Sharav both rushed out of the room only to be met by the fat spotty teenager staggering out of the bathroom looking green. They had no choice. Upstairs. Conor, with his nose still bleeding, ran after them. The boys entered what seemed to be the gang's control room. Paul frantically looked around. 'There!' He ran over to the corner of the room picking up what must be Rachel's phone. 'Grab some papers!' he said to Sharav. They both grabbed what they could and stuffed them into their pockets. Then Conor was at the door. He held his arms out blocking their exit.

'Paul, Sharav, this isn't what it looks like.' Conor was now using his Irish accent.

'Who are you anyway?' shouted Paul.

'You know who I am.'

'Stay away from us,' said Sharav.

Paul and Sharav were backing away towards the door which led to the balcony. Sharav, keeping his eyes on Conor, reached for the handle and slid the door open. They stepped out onto the balcony. Conor followed them slowly. Just then Baldy arrived at the door.

'You little…!'

'Ronnie, it's okay,' Conor interrupted in his London accent. 'I've got this.'

Baldy barged his way past Conor, moving quickly towards Paul and Sharav. Their backs were against the balcony. There was no way out.

28

SKITTLES

'YOU DRUGGED US!' Baldy spat. 'I'm going to kill you.'

Baldy looked over the edge of the balcony. He turned to them both, smiling. 'Three stories up. Do you bounce?'

He edged towards them. He grabbed Paul by the scruff and started lifting him. Paul's legs were in mid-air when Conor suddenly rushed towards Baldy, grabbing him around the neck in a sleeper hold. He was trying to cut off the blood supply to knock Baldy out. Baldy backed into Conor quickly. Conor fell backwards pulling the man with him. He managed to roll backwards as they fell, throwing Baldy over his head towards the other end of the balcony. They were both on their feet again quickly. Baldy looked confused, 'What is this, Phil?'

'Sorry Ronnie, this isn't personal.' Before Baldy could process the sentence, Conor landed a right hook into his face, knocking him back into the room. He followed him quickly. Baldy grabbed a metal lamp from the table. Wrenching the cable from the socket, he pulled the shade off and smashed the bulb so that shards of metal and glass were sticking out from the top. Conor approached him slowly as Baldy swung the lamp wildly saying, 'You won't leave this house alive.'

Conor ducked under the lamp as it swung towards his head. Then he had to jump back quickly when Baldy tried to stab him in the stomach. They were edging around the table in the middle of the room. Paul and Sharav were watching from the balcony door. Conor looked at them. 'Stay back,' he warned them. Conor's split-second distraction was enough time for Baldy to throw the lamp at him like a javelin. The broken glass stuck into Conor's leg. He staggered backwards, pulling it out slowly to reveal a large gash. Baldy laughed as he reached for a baseball bat propped up against the wall. Conor, weakened by his wound, looked around the room for a weapon. Paul and Sharav looked in disbelief as Conor fell to the floor holding his leg. He was on his back and was trying to edge away from his assailant. Baldy walked towards him wielding the bat. As he stood over Conor he said, 'Goodbye Phil or whatever your name is!'

With a sudden burst of movement, Conor twisted around on his back, pushing hard with one foot against the wall and slid fast under the table. As he was sliding, he kicked against the underside of the table, throwing it towards Baldy. The table smashed against the attacker, knocking him backwards, and he hit his head hard against the wall. Sharav and Conor looked aghast as Baldy slid down the wall unconscious.

Conor got to his feet holding his leg. He smiled at Sharav and Paul. 'Howaya lads. Right then, what's next?'

Paul walked towards him, 'You okay?'

'Grand. Listen, we should get out of here!'

Just as he said that, they heard the choppy roar of rotors. They turned and walked out onto the balcony and saw to their astonishment a black helicopter flying towards the house. It hovered over the back garden and three ropes were thrown out, followed by six heavily armed men dressed in black. 'Looks like SAS commandos,' shouted Conor over the noise.

One of the remaining soldiers in the helicopter was pointing her gun towards them and then lowered it, signalling something with her hand. She was using some sort of sign language. Conor squinted and tried to interpret, 'What's she saying... I see.... Enemy? Enemy!' Conor swung round, as did the boys, and there was Baldy, rushing towards them. Conor side-stepped, punched him in the stomach with one hand and used the other hand to throw him over the balcony. They all watched as Baldy fell three stories, smashing through the glass roof of the conservatory.

TEN MINUTES LATER Paul and Sharav were reunited with Terry in the back garden. The helicopter had landed in the park near the sea. It turned out that Terry had called for help even though he didn't hear the entire code phrase.

'Captain and his mate. It's good to see you! I mean that was awesome! Come on! We did it. Go us, go us, go us!' he chanted. 'When can we do that again. I feel... I feel all jingly and jangly... I feel amazing.' Terry was staring at them with wide eyes as he waited to hear what they had to say.

Sharav eventually said, 'It didn't feel awesome

from the inside.'

'Yeah but for me, it was like watching the best movie ever! It feels like I've eaten a thousand Skittles,' Terry said, showing them his phone. 'Oh, yeah and the only slightly disappointing thing was the bomb malfunction.'

Paul turned quickly to look at Terry. 'The bomb malfunction?'

'Yeah an explosion would have made for a great end to that bad boy of an episode.' Terry smiled.

'What bomb, Terry?' asked Paul.

'It was just a couple of pipe bombs that I decided to throw in the laundry window. You know, to shake things up a bit. I reckoned that you could do with a bit of...'

Paul rushed off to find the SAS commander. 'Commander, I think there might be a couple of bombs in there. Get your soldiers out.'

The commander looked towards the house and touched his ear, 'Fire in the hole. Abort, abort. Repeat abort, abort, fire in the hole. Over.' Once he had given that command he turned to the assembled group in the back garden. 'Everyone out!' he shouted. The commandos responded instantly and before they knew it Paul, Terry and Sharav were being closely followed by the remaining soldiers, two of whom were dragging a now semiconscious Baldy between them. They congregated beside the helicopter and turned to look at the house. They waited. The commander smiled and walked over to boys, 'Looks like a false alarm, boys. I'm really glad because the gas supply enters the building through the laundry room. Anyway, better to be….'

BOOM! The commander was interrupted by an explosion. They all watched as the windows of the house shattered. But this was only the start. There was a series of deep booming noises as the fire followed the gas pipe up into the attic and the roof was punched through by a huge, angry, orange cloud of fire. Everyone started running towards the sea. Just then, the final explosion occurred. It blew the back off the house and everyone was knocked flat. They lay there for a few seconds before the commander shouted at them to get up and keep running. As they looked behind them, they could see why. The sky was raining down with bricks, glass and stone. When they reached the sea, they looked back to see the helicopter destroyed by falling debris.

Paul and Sharav looked over at Terry, half expecting him to be shame-faced. Instead, Terry was jumping up and down shouting 'NOW, THAT'S WHAT I'M TALKING ABOUT!' He was filming it on his phone.

Forty-five minutes later the area had become significantly busier. There were countless emergency vehicles at the scene, along with a growing crowd of onlookers who were standing behind the cordon. Rob and Natalie had also arrived by helicopter. Rob talked to the SAS commander and then to the uniformed police officers who had all the gang members, including Conor, handcuffed. When Rob finished talking to the policeman, he signalled to the other officers to take the gang away. As Conor was being led away he lent down and whispered something in Paul's ear. Paul looked up in alarm and watched Conor until he was bundled into the car.

Rob walked over to the boys. 'Well lads, it's certainly good to be back in Scotland, don't you think?' No response. He continued, 'So anyone want to tell me what this was all about? Looks like some adventure.' Paul remained quiet as Sharav and Terry talked through everything that had happened. Sharav finished by saying how they managed to grab Rachel's phone and most of the papers.

'Wow, that is an amazing adventure! Better than I imagined. Well I suppose I should take the phone and get it analysed.' He put his hand out to Paul. Paul reached into his inside pocket and handed over the phone.

'Great, thank you. I'll take the papers as well. And now I think it is time we properly debriefed you back at St Andrew's House.'

Sharav and Paul hung back slightly and Sharav leaned over to Paul.

'What did Conor whisper to you, Paul?'

Paul hesitated and then whispered back, 'He said, "don't trust Rob".'

29

THE REVEAL

LATE THAT NIGHT, Paul, Sharav and Terry found themselves in the boardroom of St Andrew's House, a Scottish Government building in Edinburgh. It was a large room with an enormous oak table surrounded by expensive looking chairs. Also present, ready for the debriefing were William, Rob, Natalie, Esmee and three senior officers from MI5. Uncle Stewart was also there. He was chairing the meeting.

'Okay everyone, welcome to this debriefing where we will be discussing the events of the last number of days,' said Stewart. 'Apologies for the late meeting but it took a while to mobilise everyone to Edinburgh. You may not know everyone by name, but for security reasons I'm going to keep it like that.' He looked towards the boys and said, 'Boys, please debrief us about what happened. Provide as much detail as possible.'

Paul and Sharav took it in turns to tell everyone the full story. They explained what had motivated their decision to travel to Edinburgh and to seek Terry's help. Terry smiled broadly and simply said, 'Obviously.'

Paul told the group how they were convinced of Rachel's innocence and that they wanted to clear her name and find their father. They recalled how Terry had helped them locate her phone and recounted the events leading to the house exploding.

When they had finished, Stewart smiled and said, 'Thanks for that. Can I say your actions were brave, if a little reckless? I hope you know that you endangered not just your lives but the life of Terry, not to mention the lives of the SAS commandos who were sent to rescue you.' The boys nodded solemnly. 'You did, however, take down an extremely dangerous gang, who were clearly set on assassinating the Prime Minister.'

He looked around the table. 'Okay, now to the next point on the agenda. Where are we up to in the investigation of my niece, Rachel Fox and have we uncovered Sabre?'

Rob signalled to Esmee saying, 'The boys retrieved Rachel's phone and I passed it to Esmee for analysis.'

Esmee placed Rachel's phone on the table and shook her head saying, 'I'm terribly sorry but this phone has been wiped of all data, so it has. I tried everything I could, but I wasn't able to restore it.' She looked to Sharav and Paul, 'I'm sorry boys.'

Rob sat back in his seat. The room was silent. Then Paul pulled a different phone from his pocket and quietly pushed it towards Esmee.

'What's that, Paul?' asked his uncle.

Paul looked directly at Rob and said, 'This is Rachel's phone.'

There were gasps from a couple of people in the room. Stewart said, 'Paul, I think you'd better explain yourself.'

'I gave Rob my phone instead of Rachel's.' He turned to Esmee and said, 'Esmee, would you mind analysing this phone? Focus on the very last sound recording along with the messages.'

Esmee took the phone and connected it to her laptop. There followed a few minutes of uncomfortable silence. Finally, Esmee said, 'I think I've got something.'

She linked the phone to the screen behind her. On it she was able to display a series of messages which clearly showed all the correspondence from the people blackmailing Rachel, along with the photos of her father, Michael Fox. She then played the last recording over the room's sound system. It was a clear audio recording of the gang's discussion about Sabre. They discussed how Sabre was involved with Rachel's investigation and how Sabre was key to both the previous and the next assassination attempts on the Prime Minister.

The atmosphere in the room changed.

Paul continued, 'Conor warned me not to trust Rob. So, I gave Rob my phone instead of Rachel's. I asked Terry to track its movements. The phone was taken to a location in Edinburgh and shortly after that, the signal died.'

Everyone was now looking at Rob.

Rob smiled and said, 'Don't be ridiculous. I came straight back and handed it to Esmee. Maybe she did something to it?'

Paul's face flushed with anger, 'Our friend Terry is very clever. You see he remotely turned on the mic of my phone and recorded this audio file two minutes before the phone went dead.' He opened up a laptop in front of him and hit a key. It was Rob's voice, 'Make sure nothing can be recovered from this phone. Do you hear me?' Then another voice, 'Yes boss.'

Paul said, 'Two minutes later the phone went dead.'

Rob stood up, 'This doesn't prove anything. Someone is trying to frame me.'

Paul also stood up. Raising his voice slightly, he said, 'Rob we didn't hand you all the paper documents either. The documents we recovered from the house provided more details about Sabre. It gave us locations, meeting dates, detailed correspondence about where Sabre would be in the lead-up to the previous assassination attempt. It won't be difficult to link you to these movements and demonstrate that you are Sabre.'

Rob's face grew red. He placed his right hand near to his left wrist. He laughed manically. 'You got me. And my plan was so close to working.'

Natalie stood up. 'Rob, what do you mean? Are you really involved?'

Steward spoke quietly yet firmly. 'Rob take your

hand away from your watch, please.'

'I'm not going to prison for trying to kill that piece of dirt Prime Minister. She deserves to die. She is the one with no moral compass. When she was Foreign Secretary, she refused to rescue my brother from the Russians. My brother who sacrificed so much for his country as a spy. My brother's life was worth more than that. Way more.'

Rob's rant was interrupted by Stewart saying, 'Whole systems shut down.' Suddenly all the screens in the room switched off, along with everyone's watches. Rob looked down at his watch and started shaking with fury. He reached down and pulled a gun from his ankle. Sweeping it from left to right, he edged towards the door.

'What about my dad?' asked Paul.

Rob smiled again. 'You can't help him now. We thought we could get information out of him, but he didn't talk. My associates have instructions to kill him if they don't hear from me by sunrise. Goodbye.' He turned to go.

Natalie rushed at him and Rob swiftly swung the gun around and shot at her. He looked in shock as she fell to the floor. Then he ran out of the room.

Rob sprinted down the corridor at full speed. As he turned the corner, there was Conor. Rob didn't have time to raise his gun. Conor swiftly jumped high into the air and landed a two-footed kick to Rob's head. Rob was thrown back with huge force and landed on the floor, out cold.

30

GOODBYE, DAD

AT 8 AM TERRY and Sharav were outside St Andrew's House in the pitch dark, watching Paul pace up and down the street. They all turned as they heard the door open and there was Rachel, followed by Conor. Paul rushed towards Rachel and gave her a long hug. They briefly shared a smile.

Conor sensed their hesitancy towards him and said, 'Listen you lot, I'm on your side. I'll explain later. You did so well in uncovering Sabre and saving your sister and the Prime Minister. Well done!' He handed them all their watches. Terry looked forlorn as he realised there wasn't one for him. 'Sure, don't worry there Terry, I'll make sure you get one of those bad boys.'

Terry put his hand over his mouth trying to hide his joy and exclaimed loudly, 'All righty then!'

Paul started pacing again. 'Yes, but what about

our dad?' He looked at his watch. Rob said that he would be dead by sunrise. That's in 30 minutes.'

Conor put his head down, 'I'm sorry. We have our best people working flat out to see if the evidence you recovered can give any clues as to where he might be. They are also interrogating Rob and the gang as we speak. So far we have nothing.'

Out of the corner of his eye Paul noticed that Terry was sitting down on the pavement studying a map. Paul wondered how he could possibly be looking at a map given everything else that was going on right now.

Then Terry stood up suddenly, rummaged in his pocket and said, 'Oh, that's weird.'

Paul approached him as Terry took out a magnifying glass to look at the map of Edinburgh.

'Where did you get that map Terry?' asked Sharav.

'I took it from the incident room,' replied Terry. 'There was something odd about it and I couldn't quite work it out.'

'But that's classified, Terry. You can't take it,' said Sharav.

Terry ignored him and continued to inspect the map through the magnifying glass. 'Ah, there!' Terry pointed at the map.

Paul took a closer look but couldn't see anything. Terry handed him his magnifying glass and Paul looked carefully. The small green and red symbol came into focus. It was the same symbol they had seen on the fish tank bomb. Paul raised his head, 'Eh guys, I think Terry might have found something.' They each took a turn to view the symbol as they formed a circle around the map.

'Any more of those symbols on the map Terry?' asked Conor.

'Nope, I've checked the whole thing. That's the only one. And it's right beside the Royal Observatory on Blackford Hill.'

'It's got to be important. We need to go and have a look,' Rachel said urgently.

'Wait there,' called Conor over his shoulder as he ran off.

Two minutes later the group heard a loud rumble followed by a screech of tyres as Conor came around the corner in a red Alfa Romeo Giulia.

They all jumped into the car and Conor hit the accelerator.

'Holy moly,' cackled Terry as they were all

thrown back in their seats. 'I think I have keiched my pants!'

Paul asked his watch, 'How long until we get to the Royal Observatory?'

'Good morning,' said Hugo. 'It's about 3 miles to the Observatory. 20 minutes in traffic, but in this car, at this time, you should be there in 5 minutes. Sunrise is at 08:31 am.'

The group stayed silent as Conor sped through the narrow streets at up to 90mph. After what seemed like an age they arrived at the observatory. The observatory was an old 1800s stone building and looked striking with its two green copper domes. The car skidded to a halt and everyone threw open their doors and jumped out.

'Wait,' said Rachel. 'It's 08:21 and we don't have much time. This building is huge so we can't afford to blindly search for the next ten minutes. We need a plan. I've been thinking. Why sunrise? Don't you think it's a coincidence that this is the Royal Observatory and that they said Dad had until sunrise to live? It's got to be something to do with light.'

Terry was getting excited, 'Yep, yep, yep. Both those domes have refurbished telescopes in them.

Maybe that's where we need to look first?'

'Worth a shot,' said Paul. 'Okay, let's split up. Conor and Sharav, you go to the west dome and Rachel, Terry and I will take the east dome.' Just then Sharav collapsed to the ground and fell fast asleep. Paul rolled his eyes, 'Okay change of plan. Terry, you go with Conor. Rachel is with me.' Each group sprinted off in different directions.

Paul and Rachel slowed to a walk as they approached the blue steel door of the east dome. Paul grabbed the padlock and pulled out his lock picks.

'Do we have time for this?' asked Rachel anxiously.

'No choice,' replied Paul. 'Can you run round the tower to see if there are any windows we could break?'

Rachel returned two minutes later. 'They are all locked and have bars on the inside. Paul, it's 8:25. Six minutes.'

'It's okay, I'm almost there… just one… more… pin.' Paul pushed the final pin into place and turned the tension wrench carefully to the right.

The padlock slipped off easily and Paul pulled hard to open the heavy door. They both ran into the dark, cavernous space. Rachel spoke into her watch, 'full beam'. A strong shaft of light cut through the darkness to reveal a copper dome 45 feet above them. A solid blue metal structure sat in the middle of the room housing a large telescope which pointed upwards.

'Dad?' Rachel's quiet voice echoed upwards. There was no response.

'Dad, are you here?' called Paul more loudly, as they walked slowly towards the central metal structure. They walked around the metal frame and scanned the periphery of the room. Nothing.

'He's not here,' said Rachel.

'Something must be here. Keep looking. Four minutes.'

They searched the room high and low using their watch lights. Finally Rachel noticed something move halfway up the metal structure. 'Paul, up there!'

Paul shone his watch to where Rachel was pointing. More movement. They scrambled up the structure as fast as they could. And there was their Dad, his eyes wide open, tears flowing down his face. Paul and Rachel embraced him. His mouth was taped, his legs were tied and his arms were handcuffed separately behind him so that he was leaning back facing the roof. Paul pulled back from the embrace and looked at his father's face. His dad was trying to say something through the tape. Paul pulled the tape from his mouth and Michael Fox said, 'Paul, Rachel, I thought I was never going to see you again! What time is it?'

'It's 8:29, Dad, we found you in time,' said Paul.

'Oh no son, you don't understand. They injected me with some sort of chemical 12 hours ago. It means that if my skin is exposed to UV rays from the sun, I will have a severe allergic reaction and die. It's too late, my beautiful children. The dome is timed to open at 8:31. But at least…'

Before Mr Fox had finished speaking, Paul was clambering up the structure towards the dome shutters. He climbed with extraordinary speed and agility across the telescope and flung himself towards the shutters. He landed on a ledge and held on precariously to a metal handle. He shuffled away from the central point towards the mechanism that would open the shutter.

'We need something to jam in these cogs!' he shouted down.

Rachel was working desperately to pick the handcuffs. She quickly scanned the room and called back, 'Paul, there isn't anything here.'

Paul considered all his options. Where was the timer? Could he hold the shutters closed himself? Could they move Dad in time? No, there was no time. His stomach lurched as he heard the mechanism grumble into action. It was too late. He checked his watch, 08:31.

'Rachel, its opening!'

'I can't get the handcuffs open Paul,' she cried. She leant down and kissed her father on the forehead. 'Goodbye Dad, I love you.'

'I love you, Rachel,' Michael replied. 'It's okay Paul, come down and see me.'

Just then, as Paul had lost all hope, he had an idea. He threw the only thing that he had to hand toward the mechanism. There was a horrible screeching, grinding noise as the mechanism slowed and then stopped.

Conor and Terry ran in through the door and looked up at Paul, who was illuminated by Rachel's watch. Sharav followed them, looking groggy.

'How did you stop it?' called Rachel.

'I've thrown my watch into the cogs,' said Paul loudly as he started climbing down. 'It won't hold for long. Conor, climb up and help us.'

Rachel managed to get one of the handcuffs off, while Conor worked on the second one. Paul untied his dad's feet. Soon Michael Fox was free and was climbing down to the ground. When they reached the ground, he grabbed both Paul and Rachel and held them close. After a minute, there was a loud crack and they all looked up towards the shutters. The watch had finally succumbed, and the mechanism was slowly pulverising the watch. Rachel pointed at a small office in the corner of the room and Mr Fox was rushed towards it. Paul pulled Sharav's jacket from him and threw it over the only window of the office just as the shutters finally opened, flooding the observatory with bright morning sunlight.

31

RESTORED

THREE DAYS LATER Paul, Sharav and Rachel were hanging out in MI2 headquarters on the blue level. Paul and Rachel were swinging on a couple of hammocks, while Sharav was sitting on the floor, leaning against one of the pineapple pods. They were spending time recounting some of their adventures and Rachel wanted to hear all about how they tracked down her phone.

She laughed and listened open-mouthed as the boys retold their story, describing Terry's heroic actions and how he had managed to stay calm, most of the time. Rachel's favourite part of the story was how the different gang members were affected by the drugs. The boys were busily recounting the house explosion when behind them they heard a familiar Irish accent.

'How's it going, lads?'

They turned around to see a smiling Conor striding towards them.

'Howaya? You recovered from all the stuff last week?'

'We're okay, I think,' said Paul, whose head was still full of questions. Paul still wasn't sure whether they could fully trust Conor. He decided to go for it. 'Conor, I don't know where to start. How about, we can't believe you're alive! Sharav and I saw you fall into the sea. No one was found. I mean, was that planned?'

'That, my friend, is a great place to start,' said Conor pulling himself up into a free hammock. 'Okay no, it wasn't planned but it was a great opportunity! I didn't know that man would be on the ship but falling overboard with him was the only way of keeping you safe, Paul. Anyway, remember the shots that were fired? Well, the bullets didn't hit me. I think they hit the other bloke because I didn't see him come back up again. When you're in the sea, your top priority is to stay afloat. It was pretty calm out there, so I lay on me back and floated. I was wondering what to do when I remembered my mentor saying to me, "The most effective spies are the ones that are invisible." I hoped that you would raise the alarm and that a team would come looking for me, but I needed everyone to think that I was dead. When I was a teenager, I learnt to hold me breath for up to four minutes.'

'Wow,' said Sharav smiling.

'Anyway, I saw the rescue craft coming for me, so I dived under the surface. I needed to be careful that I didn't get chopped to pieces by the propellers and I just managed to grab on to the underside of the boat as it went past. Every couple of minutes or so I would risk putting me head above the surface to get some air. I was so close to the boat but they didn't think about looking over the sides. I was freezing by then but thankfully after 45 minutes they headed back to the ship. I managed to cling on to the boat as it was pulled out of the water. It's a long story but I stowed away in the rescue vessel and got off the ship when we docked in Pembroke.'

Rachel stared at him, 'But why did you not want to be found?'

Conor sat up in the hammock and looked at her. 'I took the chance to use the best cover ever. You know, death.'

'But why did you need the cover?' asked Sharav.

'Ah good question. Well you know, Irish Intelligence have been working with the UK security services for years. Me included. I had my suspicions that MI5 and MI2 had a mole. In fact, my suspicions were pretty specific. I had worked with Rob on a couple of missions in Ireland and although I couldn't put me finger on it at first, things weren't quite right. I'm not used to missions failing, but when I worked with Rob, they went wrong all the time. Both missions failed. Really important ones. There was nothing concrete, but sure I knew it in my bones. So when I got off the boat at Pembroke, I contacted me boss Mary O'Connell and told her what was going on. She was fine with the plan. Mary put a trace on all Rob's calls and there was one number we couldn't identify. That number was tracked to North Berwick. So off I went, and with the help of some of my dodgy contacts I was recommended to Ronnie, you know the bald gang leader.' Conor continued, 'Ronnie takes a while to trust people. He had his inner circle and I had only just shown up. I was just beginning to find out some information and work out a bit more about Rob's treachery. I had heard the name "Sabre" and was wondering if that was Rob. You lot got to it first. A more direct route I suppose!'

Rachel looked up, 'So that gang were the ones blackmailing me?'

'Afraid so,' said Conor. 'From what I've worked out this particular cell wanted to cause as much disruption to the country as possible. To totally destabilise it in fact. They had two missions. They wanted to get top secret information out of a very senior spy, so they kidnapped your dad. However, when they realised that he wasn't going to talk they decided to capture one of his children. That would have been the best way to make him talk. They didn't manage to do that, so they continued with their other mission. To kill the Prime Minister. And to be fair they quite cleverly used your dad to blackmail you into doing their bidding.'

Rachel put her head down, 'I know. That was close!'

Paul said, 'Yeah but Rachel, I would have done the same thing in your shoes. Anyway, I can't believe they used a thirteen-year-old!'

'I know but these men are ruthless,' said Conor. 'They used Rob's hate of the Prime Minister. Rob blames her personally for the death of his brother. But the PM wouldn't have risked a war with Russia for the sake of rescuing one agent. Probably the right decision.'

Conor turned to Paul and Rachel. 'Oh yeah, Paul and Rachel, your dad said he wanted a quick chat. One at a time if possible.'

Paul looked at Rachel, who nodded. He jumped down from the hammock and walked towards the moonstone office. As he entered, he saw that a new ceiling had been installed that blocked out the light.

They sat on either side of the oak desk, on which a new watch lay. It was turned off.

'How are you, Dad?'

'Much better, son. The UV light thing is still a problem, but we have some great scientists trying to come up with a drug to reverse the condition. I'm hopeful. But in the meantime, I'm spending a lot of time in here. I can move around at night so that's not too bad.'

'Oh, that's good,' replied Paul. 'You're looking better.'

Michael Fox smiled. 'Paul, I'm proud of you. You've been through a lot over the last couple of years. And despite all that, you've shown amazing levels of character and resilience. No matter what happens, no matter what choices you make, I want you to know that I love you and want to be a better dad. I'm sorry for failing you, Rachel and your mum.'

Paul looked directly into his dad's tear-filled, blue eyes. 'Okay, Dad. It's okay.'

His father heaved a long sigh and pointed towards the watch. 'Paul, it's time for you to choose whether to stay at MI2 and complete your training. But before you decide I've got something else to tell you. I think if I'm going to be a better dad to you and Rachel, I need to be open with you and tell you one more thing. It's about your sister Kate.'

Paul felt the stab of pain in his stomach and shifted in his chair, saying quietly, 'Okay.'

'Yeah. Well listen. You know she died in a car accident. The thing is… this is really hard to say.'

'Tell me, Dad.'

'Paul, the brakes didn't fail. We didn't hit a wall. A truck hit us. But the driver was never found. It was late and we were driving on a country road.' Michael paused for a moment. 'MI5 investigated it. The driver disappeared but he made a mistake. He left some documents in the cab of his truck. There was a picture of our car, a note of our registration and details of where we were going that night. Paul, it wasn't an accident. The target was probably me, but the truth is your sister was murdered.'

Paul stared at his father and watched as tears fell from his eyes, making tiny splashes on the desk. 'Paul, I loved her so much. She was taken from us that night. And I can't rest until I find who did it. I won't stop.' He wiped his eyes with a tissue and looked up again. 'Paul, you can walk away. I promise to spend more time with you and Rachel regardless of your decision. It's your choice.'

Paul stood up and walked round the desk. He leaned down to his father and hugged him tightly. He then stood up and turned to face the door. Pausing beside the desk, he grabbed the watch and started walking. Without turning round, he said, 'I'm in.'

Dear Reader,

I really hope you enjoyed the adventure! I would love to hear what you thought about the book. You can do this by leaving a review on Amazon or by visiting my website where you will also find news, interviews and information about the Paul Fox Spy Adventures.

Thanks for reading.
Glenn

www.glenncarterauthor.com